Consume – A Devou

Consume

A Devoured Novel

Book Two

Shelly Crane

Editing services provided by Jennifer Nunez.

Printed 2012 for paperback, Kindle and E-book format through Amazon, Create Space and Barnes & Noble.
Cover models: Shali and Jason Geiger

More information can be found at the author's website
http://shellycrane.blogspot.com/

ISBN-13: 978-1475199093
ISBN-10: 1475199090

Acknowledgements

A gigantic, humungous thank you to

Jennifer N, Gloria G, Mandy A, Amanda C, Shali Geiger, Georgia Cates, Quinn Loftis, Angeline Kace, Samantha Young, Amy Bartol, Catherine Moore and my Twitter and Facebook pals for always being available, for always being real and upfront with me, for always saying 'That sucks, dude!' or 'That's awesome!' because an author definitely needs to hear both at certain times. For being helpful and sweet and the cherry on top of the sundae that is my life!

I love you and need you. Ever grateful!

To my hubs, Axel, you're still amazing and I love you.

Infinity

"A person often meets his destiny on the road he took to avoid it."

-Jean de La Fontaine

One

I felt wretched as I walked away from Tate's house. His mom hadn't let me in to see him, which really was fine with me. I just wanted to drop off some pamphlets. Last night at the carnival, Tate just seemed distraught on a new level. So I researched a recovery program for kids who were having problems with drugs or steroids that didn't have any support from family or friends. I thought that fit Tate's situation pretty nicely.

So I went down to the center this morning, picked up some pamphlets and put them in an envelope. I knew that Tate had told his parents I dumped him. Or he probably said it was him who had done the dumping. I'm sure the story was something ugly that I had done because his mom basically snatched the envelope - that I said was a school project - and then slammed the door in my face.

I asked Eli to let me go alone, for obvious reasons; an altercation with Tate right now wasn't going to solve anything for any of us. I wasn't trying to give Tate false hope by helping him; he just used to be my friend. He used to be my boyfriend. He used to be a good guy, and he had helped me through the worst time in my entire life. So, I thought it was only fair and right to try to help him, though I doubted he was going to take the advice. I could hope.

I twisted my dark hair to the side of my neck and let the spring sun beat down on me. It was almost summer, almost prom, almost graduation, almost a new life for me in every conceivable way.

A face suddenly nuzzling my neck from behind and arms around me made me smile. I turned in his arms to see the purple eyes that looked at me with love that we never spoke out loud. "Hey."

"Hey, you," he said and with a hand on my jaw, he pulled my face up to kiss me. "How did it go?" he asked, but he covered my lips with his again refusing to let me answer. He knew just what to do and how to do it to render speech an impossibility. I leaned back, forcing him to groan in complaint. "I don't really care how good old Tate is doing," he informed me. "I was just being polite."

"I know that," I said. "And I'm grateful that you *allowed me* to see him," I spouted sarcastically. "But I felt I owed it to him."

He sighed and rubbed his hand down my arm to my wrist, to the bond. He caressed it lovingly, and whether he knew what he was doing to me or not wasn't clear. "I know, and as much as I hate to admit it, I'm pretty grateful to Tate for taking good care of you before I got here."

I knew what he meant. I told him all about Tate last night and how he helped me when my parents died. We rode the Ferris wheel with Patrick a couple of times, and then by ourselves. We didn't get off. It was as good a place to talk as any, so we just kept riding, over and over. We talked about everything, but the Horde and Hatch. Well, I talked.

Eli was interested in what my life had been like without him, without Pastor and Mrs. Ruth's influence and care for me. I told him all about my parents and my sister and how I was a mere shadow of the girl I'd been before.

He held me as we watched the city make a loop under us, the Ferris wheel the only thing that seemed to hold us to the earth. He hummed a nameless song that deliciously haunted my dreams last night. I eventually had one of those epiphany moments this morning in the shower and realized it was 'Paradise' by Coldplay, and got shampoo in my eyes as I stood there trying to remember the words.

"I know," I told him. "But you're here now, and I've done my deed for Tate. Now we just have to worry about trying to finish high school."

"You mean *you* have to worry about finishing," he corrected and grinned. "I'm not even technically registered here."

"So," I thought, "how many times have you technically graduated?"

"None," he said and grimaced. "I always left before graduation. Dresses and I don't mesh well."

I laughed and shook my head. "It's not a dress. It's a gown."

"And what's the definition for 'gown' in the dictionary?"

"Ok, fine," I surrendered. "Are you at least going to watch me in my dress?"

He gave me a puzzled look. "Of course I am. I wouldn't miss it for anything, and I'm not going anywhere without you."

"Good," I whispered. I watched him lace our fingers between us; the barbed string attached to us both seemed to hum at his attention. He slowly inched his way back to my lips, pulling me up as he did so. He captured my mouth in a slow and lazy motion that had me digging my fingers into his shoulders. Something seemed to change between us last night. After he saved me, after all the Horde and carnival stuff, we seemed different. For one, I'd never been so caressed and devoured with someone's eyes before without even touching. And when he added the touching…like now…it was a whole new ball game for me.

I slipped my hand into the collar of his black button up shirt and inched my hand to the back of his neck. When his lips left mine, I was sure I whined, but then I didn't do anything at all as his mouth made it to my chin, and then my jaw, and then the side of my neck. I felt the warm metal of his tongue ring and exhaled an embarrassingly loud breath into his hair. I swore I felt his lips smile.

And then an annoyance worse than an alarm clock blared near us. "Eew! Seriously?"

Eli growled his irritation against my skin and turned to look at Deidre. No matter the differences that were so blatantly attached to Eli and me, Deidre apparently hadn't changed. My little speech hadn't broken any barriers of her conscience. Eli spat his words to her. "I suggest you walk on."

"What? Done with me, so now you think you have to protect Clara?"

"I had to have you first to be done with you," he rebutted. "And Clara didn't need any of my help dealing with you last night."

Deidre huffed. "You weren't even there. Hearsay doesn't count."

"Oh, I was there." He laughed softly and pulled me closer, his arm possessive and intimate around my waist. "Better scurry along or you'll be late," he told her as he turned back to me. He smiled before kissing me once more on the lips. We heard her shiny flats padding away angrily on the sidewalk. "We better go, too."

"Yeah," I agreed. We started to walk and he grabbed my hand as we crossed the street. The sun was bright and overly warm for so early in the morning. It beat down on my jacket and then crested in a blinding arc over the top of the school as we approached as if welcoming us in.

High school. Only a few weeks to go and it would all be history. Good riddance.

~ ~ ~

The bell came and went as I slammed my locker shut. Math book in hand I looked up to Eli and smiled as I saw his face etching a path to mine. I accepted his easy kiss and smiled as I turned to head to homeroom.

Floating on a cloud I felt lighter than I'd felt in days. I sank into my seat in homeroom, not even glancing Tate's way, and said my 'Here' when roll call was in full swing. I rested my chin on my hand and tried to act normal, when all I really wanted to do was crash through the door and get back to my Eli.

What was wrong with me?

This was pretty crazy. I definitely had to label myself as the boy-crazy girl I'd been borderlined as before. I was no longer borderline. I was full-fledged, dreamy sighs and proneness to daydreams included.

The bell jerked me from my thoughts and I looked up at to see everyone piling out of the classroom. I grabbed my stuff and stood, only to bump into someone…Tate. Great.

"Hey, Clara," he said oddly.

"Tate," I answered back evenly. I wasn't looking to get into an altercation, and if he was fishing, I'd throw the bait back at him.

"I got your envelope this morning…and, uh…" He cleared his throat exceptionally long. I looked up at his face and tried to keep the pity to a minimum. "I just… What were you thinking?"

"What?" I asked in a flurry as his sudden change in tone.

He crossed his arms over his chest and glared at me. "My dad could have intercepted your little *present* and then I'd have really been in it deep."

"I was trying to help you. You helped me…when I really needed it." My voice went all soft and sympathetic. I reined it in as his face lost some of its tightness. "I just wanted to return the favor. You need help, Tate."

"I…I know," he admitted to the floor. "I just… I just don't know where to start."

"Where to start would be telling your parents."

Back to square one. His jaw tightened and he jammed his hands into his pockets. "No way. I'll be fine. I really don't see why you're so worried about me anyway."

"I told you. I felt like I owed you."

"I wasn't nice to you so you'd help me hide my addiction later, Clara," he said harshly.

"I know that," I told him with certainty. I didn't say anything else. The person had to want to change. It couldn't be forced. And from the way his nose was scrunching, the change wasn't coming today.

"Please just stay out of my business," he said and walked around me. I heard him mutter as he kept walking. "Especially since you don't belong to me anymore."

Ok. I took a deep breath and realized this was what I thought was going to happen. He admitted it at least, but wasn't looking for a fork in the road. I had done my deed and felt good. Maybe one day he'd come around, but for now, I was free of him and any guilt that I may have felt. Though it was totally stupid to feel guilty over any of it.

Done. With. It.

I bumped into someone as I scrambled for my next class. I apologized and started to leave, but they grabbed my sleeve.

"Hey," she said.

"Oh, hey, Ariel." I stopped and looked at her. "Are you ok? Pat said you were sick or something last night."

"I'm fine," she said, but she totally wasn't. Her eyes were black underneath, and not from any Goth look she was rocking. She hadn't slept at all and I felt terrible because I knew why.

"Hey, you want to have a sleepover or something tonight?" I blurted out in my newfound need to try to fix things. I was no longer going to sit on the sidelines while things happened around me.

"Really?" she said stunned. I nodded. "Ok," she answered quickly. "My parents have been out of town for a few days. They come back tomorrow night so that's perfect."

No wonder she didn't sleep last night. After Demarcus has scared the crap out of her, and there was no logical explanation for it, she'd gone home to an empty house. "Great! It's settled. Vamp show marathon, here we come!" I said excitedly. I *was* actually excited and it wasn't all for her benefit! My other friends never slept over or did anything like that with me. I was always alone in my Salvatore\Spike\Angel obsession. Until now.

Her eyes seemed to brighten a bit, her pallor and color becoming a thing of the past. I looked at her objectively for probably the first time. The nose ring connected to her earring was intimidating to say the least, but at least she rocked it. The short hair she had sported since I could remember did bring out her cheek bones, for real. She wasn't thin, but wasn't heavy either, her curves showing through her skirt, unlike mine. Our feet were total contrasts to each other; my petite ballet flats and her big black boots.

I smiled. She was my complete opposite. A foot in the right direction away from the guarded years of pretending to be something I wasn't.

"Come on," I said. "Who do you have next?"

"Smith." She drawled and popped a piece of chewing gum into her mouth and grinned. "He hates it when I chew gum."

I laughed as I glanced around for Eli. I spotted him watching me, leaning against the lockers with his hip. He was smirking. "Lunch," I called to Ariel and waved over my shoulder.

"Mos def!"

I pushed my way through the throngs and liked it a lot when he opened his arms to me. I went and almost slammed into him as the masses scrammed to make it to class before the bell. He caught me easily and pulled me to the side as if to protect me from the herd. "It's crazy today," he muttered.

"Yeah," I agreed halfheartedly because my excitement and focus were definitely elsewhere now. "So, Ariel's coming to spend the night with me."

"She is?" His voice was high with surprise.

"Yeah. Her parents come back tomorrow night, but she didn't sleep at all last night because of what that," I looked around for listening ears, "Devourer did to her."

He nodded his head in recognition. "Ok," he said slowly. "Does that mean you don't want me to come to you tonight?" His voice went ground level and he inched closer. "In a reverie?"

My stupid teenage girl heart started to flutter just like butterfly wings. Just like in those books that Ariel reads. I wanted to curse it and be mad at it, but Eli's breath hit my cheek and all thoughts of insignificant things left me. "No, you can come to me," I said breathlessly. "I want you to."

"Good," he answered, his voice almost a growl. He kissed my cheek and then turned me. He pushed me gently on the small of my back with both hands and said, "Bell's in eighteen seconds. Go fast."

I turned to look at him as I almost sprinted down the hall. He was watching me to as he walked into his class. I thought he'd bump right into the wall because he never once looked up to see where he was going. But he walked right into his class door, and his eyes disappeared.

I didn't have the same luck.

I banged my shin on a small metal trash can keeping my class door open. It resounded around the room and hall as I tried not to howl. "Ow," I muttered and ignored the couple of idiots who laughed.

"Right on time," my teacher said and then the bell rang starting another class.

Another meaningless cycle. I couldn't concentrate or focus or think. Everything just seemed so mediocre, miniscule and pointless now. Didn't these people know there was more to life than this? There were monsters out there. There was a great big ol' world with all sorts of things in it that didn't give a flip whether we passed High School Spanish or not.

They'd kill you all the same.

Two

Classes dragged, people were the same. No one seemed too interested that I wasn't hanging with the same crew anymore, and I was glad. I had enough drama to fill up daytime television and wasn't looking for more. But lunch was coming and I knew - just knew - we wouldn't come out without some kind of altercation.

Eli met me at the lunch doors, took my bag from me, and walked me in with a graceful, strong arm around my waist. He plopped all of our stuff down on Patrick's table and then proceeded me through the line. Nachos. Yay...

Pat and the rest of them soon followed and we were all laughing and sitting close around our little round table. Though Eli was fully engrossed in a conversation with Patrick about a new motorcycle he wanted to buy, Eli's hand never left my thigh. He moved and caressed with his hand every few minutes to let me know that he could be in two places at once in his mind.

Ariel and I on the other hand were just listening. And I was being enlightened an awful lot. Number one: Ariel was freaking in love with Patrick.

Number two: Patrick was a clueless fool. Number three: I wasn't the only one who noticed Ariel's penchant for the group's fearless leader. Eli tried repeatedly to ask what Ariel thought, but she just shrugged and Patrick just kept going. He did however keep a steady eye on Sarah. I felt bad for Ariel…and Patrick. No matter how much attention he showed Sarah, no matter that she had a crush on him forever, her reputation was the most important thing to her and for some reason, she was convinced that it all revolved around Dee. It didn't of course, but I didn't see Sarah coming to that realization anytime soon.

So I tried to engage Ariel in another chat to distract her, but the bell rang. We all made our way down the hall to our classes. Eli asked the kid next to me in Math – asked, not used Devourer persuasion – if he could switch seats with him. He was fine with it and now Eli was my new neighbor. Which was fine with me because I sucked at Math.

Math and I were not on speaking terms.

~ ~ ~

In Art, we were supposed to paint today. Grrr. Paint and I weren't on speaking terms either. I never left painting with my clothes unscathed, no matter the amount of protective clothing. As I slipped my apron on, I laughed a little out loud at Eli. His apron was purple, making his eyes so much brighter, but not matching. He was glorious with his uniform on and apron, all ready for teacher's instructions.

"What's so funny, Miss Hopkins?" he said and quirked a pierced brow while continuing to attempt the tie of the apron. "You laughing at me?"

"Let me do it," I said with fake disgust. I tied it loosely and stayed close when he turned.

"Thanks," he breathed. "So, where do you want to go tonight?"

I knew he meant in the reverie. "Surprise me."

"Do you mean that?" He grinned. "Because there're lots of places that I've never taken you that I'd like to." I must've looked confused so he clarified. "They have nothing to do with this po-dunk town."

"Aah," I trailed off. "Well then take me away, Calgon. I'm game."

"Calgon?"

"Never mind." I smiled. "Something my mom used to say."

"Ok," he said softly. "I'll surprise you then. But you'll have to stay awake after Ariel goes to sleep."

"Or you could just come over and watch vamp shows with us," I suggested, but I could practically mouth his rebuttal.

"Girls and vamp shows? No thanks." He played with the ball in his tongue ring with his teeth for a second. "But you gals have fun," he said sarcastically.

"We will," I retorted and bumped his hip with mine. "We don't need the likes of Eli Thames to have a fantabulous time," I spouted as I pulled my plastic gloves on.

"I'm offended," he said and held a green gloved hand to his heart. I laughed loudly just as the teacher turned. She glared at me with her precisely manicured eyebrows and I cringed in embarrassment. She always caught me doing crap in her class.

Eli chuckled. I straightened and went to stand at attention at my side of the desk, waiting for instruction. After that I sat and watched Eli as he started on -no doubt- another masterpiece.

~ ~ ~

Ariel met me eagerly at my locker. She lived near me somewhere, so she said she'd run home and meet me at my house in a few minutes. I agreed, and after stuffing my books into my locker, I slammed the door. The noise was so loud, resounding painfully in my ears.

I covered them with my hands and waited for the ringing to pass. It did after a few seconds and I looked around to see if anyone else had heard it. Everyone just walked around me and acted normally. Weird.

I brushed it off and headed for the street. Eli said he'd let me and Ariel hang out and didn't come walk me home. He said the bird was acting strangely anyway and he wanted to get home as soon as possible.

So I headed home. I walked passed Mike. Some freshman girl was eating up his attention and just thankful to be in his general vicinity. I rolled my eyes and he yelled at my back. "Got a problem, Miss Goody Goody?"

"Nope," I yelled over my shoulder and waved flippantly.

I looked back to the street and was blinded. I squinted and threw my hand up to shield my eyes, but my eyes still burned and hurt. I turned and even felt myself crouch down. Then it stopped, just like that. I looked up and around, but no one was acting different. A couple of people were looking at *me* though, and I felt like a freak. Something was going on with me. I stood quickly to bolt across the street.

I didn't look in my haste.

The car didn't have a chance to stop before it was too late. I closed my eyes, waiting for the impact...

It never came.

I looked up and saw the car had stopped. The woman's face behind the windshield was frozen in her fear of hitting someone. I turned in a slow circle to see that everyone else has frozen, too. No one moved, no one breathed, no one blinked.

I was so confused until I felt a presence behind me. I turned around quickly and was met with a boy, his face covered in the shadows of the oak tree he was standing under. It reminded me so much of when Eli had first started invading my consciousness. He had always hidden himself in shadow...

"Who are you?" I asked, because just standing there staring at him seemed a little unproductive.

"My name is whatever you want it to be," he said sweetly. "What's your name?"

"Somehow, I think you already know."

He laughed a deep chuckle. "Clever girl. You are Clara. Nice to meet you. I'm Finn, and you almost passed out on the sidewalk, Clara."

"What?" I looked around and saw nothing or no one but him and me. "How do you know that?"

I could hear the smile in his voice when he said, "Call me *Mister Know It All.*"

"This is a reverie," I realized.

His body visibly tensed. "How do you know what a reverie is?"

I thought about how to answer that. Something was going on. "You're a Devourer, aren't you? And this is a reverie? Eli won't like you going into my head, you know."

He cursed and turned quickly, punching the tree trunk. "Eli, you idiot," he said quietly.

"How do you know him?" I asked, but I knew exactly how.

"Let's just say that I'm looking for him," he drawled and stepped out of the shadows. He was a pretty guy, with thick lashes and creamy skin. "Tell Eli for me will you?"

I noticed he had no accent and no piercings. He wasn't snarky either. He was different for a Devourer. "Sure," I said and immediately came aware on the sidewalk. I was still crouched there and breathing deeply to keep from passing out. Just like he said.

I glanced up to see Eli running across the quad and parking lot. There were a few people who had stopped to stare at me, but no one asked me if I was ok. The closer Eli got, the more I could see his anger.

"Show's over," he growled to everyone. "Or you could just stand around like idiots and stare at her instead of helping her!" he shouted just as he reached me. That got people's feet moving.

He didn't crash into me. He slowed just in time to ease himself into my personal space. He gathered my face in his hands gently. "What's the matter, baby?"

I couldn't help it, I grinned. He looked confused by that and asked, "Did you hit your head?"

"No," I said through a small laugh. "You called me baby. You've never called me that before."

He smirked, but tried to tame it down. "Come on. What happened?"

"I met a guy named Finn-"

"Finn was here!" he almost shouted. He smiled, like he was truly happy about something. "Where? What happened?"

"He said to tell you he was looking for you."

"He talked to you and then just left?"

"No. He told me in the reverie I had when I-"

Eli was no longer smiling. I stopped speaking because I was confused by the sudden contained rage on his face. "He brought you into a reverie?"

"Yeah," I thought back, "he pulled me in when I got blinded by the sun. But it wasn't just being blinded it was painful and way too bright to just be that." I shook my head. "Anyway, I crouched down to stop the pain and when I did, he pulled me in. I didn't know it though and he made me think I was going to be hit by a car before everyone froze, and then they all disappeared."

"I can't believe he did that to you," he growled. I looked up at him with confusion on my face. He grasped my arms gently, bringing me closer to him. "And no one gets your reveries anymore, but me."

The old me, the snarky and spoiled and better-than-everybody me, would have tossed my hair at him and sent him a sympathy giggle before vacating the premises. The new me? The one where Eli was attached to me, literally, and could make my body respond in ways that Tate never dreamed about? She was practically a pool at Eli's feet.

I basically just held on when he leaned in to kiss me, but he pecked my lips sweetly and hugged me to him. "Finn was my only friend in this whole world. And if he's here, then things are about to get bad for us."

"But why? He wouldn't just visit you?"

"No," he answered and leaned back to inspect me, his eyes roaming. "Now, what happened? You almost passed out. That's probably what the bright light was for. Have you been feeling bad?"

"No," I said truthfully, but then realized, things had been a little weird. "Well, my ears were hurting earlier, and I kind of have a headache now."

He nodded. "Let's get you to your house and get your some aspirin. You've probably got an ear infection or something."

"But I haven't been swimming or anything."

"Well, it's got to be something, Clara," he insisted, his accent extra potent. "Come on."

As he put an arm around my waist to guide me, he looked both ways, always the ever-careful boy, and then crossed the street. He didn't knock, just went straight in and right to the kitchen. He sat me down at the kitchen table and asked Mrs. Ruth where the aspirin was. She told him and eyed me curiously as Eli got the pills and a glass of water.

He squatted down in front of me, handed me the pills and raised his eyebrow in waiting for me to take them. I rolled my eyes and took the pills. He smiled at me and then told Mrs. Ruth that I had a headache and he was taking me to my room.

She nodded to say her acceptance, but still watched me strangely. I was sure she was wondering why I was letting Eli guide me around and shove medicine at me. I frowned as we shuffled down the hall.

Had I lost my spunk?

"What on earth are you thinking so hard about?" he said as he held my door open for me.

"Nothing," I muttered and turned to him. I bumped my nose into his chest as he was so close, or he bumped into me I should say. I looked up at him and any weirdness I felt seemed trivial. He looked tortured and I didn't understand why.

"Clara," he sighed and grasped my jaw, almost as if to choke me, but his fingers were gentle and careful. And my breaths came faster. He moved us just like that to the closet door, my back barely bumping it. "How's the head now?"

"Forgotten," I breathed.

"And the ears? Still painful?" he asked, his middle finger snaking up to circle my ear.

I shivered. "What ears?"

He laughed softly. "I'm serious. Tell me what happened out there. All of it."

I dug through my muddled brain for the answers and eventually could tell him what happened. I told him about my ears hurting, the slamming locker being so incredibly loud, then the bright light and the reverie, and Finn.

He shook his head and he stared at the wall behind me head. "Something spooked Finn. He'd never come looking for me otherwise."

"Where do you know him from?"

He sighed, his breath washing my face in warmth. "He was the only other Devourer I'd ever met who understood...well, understood isn't a good word. Sympathized, I guess. He dislikes what he is, but he hasn't had some revelation like me to push him into being good. Or trying to be. I met him at the Consumed Club in Arequipa."

"Consumed Club?"

"A club where Devourers go to…mingle." He rolled his eyes angrily. "It's a place where Devourers and their mates can hang without worrying about any humans seeing anything they shouldn't."

"And you used to hang out at these clubs?" I asked softly.

His thumb swept across my lips before settling once more on my jaw line. "Yes," he answered honestly. "I used to be a Devourer just like the rest of them."

"But you never had a mate, right?"

"No."

I felt myself sigh. "So Finn is a…what? You say he's different from them, but he pulled me into a reverie and tried to scare me."

"He must have been testing you. He couldn't see the string in the reverie," he realized and looked at the one attached to his wrist. "The reverie was his making, and he doesn't know about our bond. That may be good for us, then." He seemed to relax a bit. "If he doesn't know about it like I thought, then maybe word hasn't gotten out yet."

"I'm sorry that you're stuck here with me," I said and wished I was older, wiser, more capable of taking care of myself.

"No," he said and shook his head. "No." He moved in easily and right as I sucked in a breath, ready for our lips to connect, the doorbell rang.

"Crap. Ariel," I told him.

He made a noise like a growl in his throat. "Horrible timing, Ariel."

I smiled at him. "Come to me later."

"Oh, I will. Get her to go to bed soon."

Three

I laughed. He moved his hand to the back of my neck. "You're sure you're alright? After everything that happened today?"

"I'm fine, I promise."

He tilted my chin and kissed me, speaking against my mouth. "I can't lose you."

He started to pull away, but I felt him stop, hesitate. Then he pressed closer and forced my mouth open with his in a rare show of being a little out of control of his perfect reins. His hand released my neck and he pulled me to him with gripping, desperate hands.

I recognized this display for what it was. He was scared. He couldn't be with me every second and that friend of his, Finn, could have just as easily been someone who wasn't a friend. I could have been really hurt, and I got that, but what Eli didn't get was that that could have happened to me even I wasn't with him. Devourers were everywhere, cars were everywhere, drunk drivers were everywhere, accidents happened. My parents were proof of that.

There was no way to save me from life. He was afraid he was going to lose me, and in truth he was. One day I'd get old and die, or have an untimely accident before then, and he was going to lose me. Maybe he was just now understanding that.

And I guess that I hadn't really understood that either until just now.

I wrapped my arms around his neck and went to my tiptoes, urging him to lift me, pull me closer. And just as I felt his hands going to the backs of my thighs to do just that, a startled noise reached my ears and it hadn't come from me.

Eli and I both jerked our eyes to the door, without letting go, to see an entertained Ariel as she pressed her lips together and toed the floor with her boot to keep from laughing. "Woops."

I smiled in embarrassment and released Eli, but he didn't release me. He leaned forward to my ear, his lips skimming my skin as he whispered. "I'll see you in a bit. Don't trust anyone, not even Finn. If you get pulled into a reverie, just pretend to do what they want until they release you, ok? Don't let them know that you know about us." He pulled back to see if I'd agree, but shot a quick glance at Ariel and then smirked down at me to make Ariel think he was talking dirty to me instead of fearing for my life.

"Yes, babe," I said sweetly and with true, pure sincerity, "I promise."

His looked morphed to adoration and satisfaction before he kissed me once more, then sighed as he released me slowly. He made his way to the door and tipped his head to Ariel. "Ariel," he said dryly to show her his amused annoyance with her for interrupting us.

"Eli," she retorted. We listened to his footsteps and then heard the door shut. She laughed as she bounced to me. "Holy guacamole! That was hot, Clara."

"Yeah," I agreed and touched my lips in awe. The promise ring on my finger practically stared me down in disappointment. "I didn't do anything," I told it quietly.

"Huh?" she asked and I realized she'd heard me.

"Nothing. You want snacks?"

"Shyeah!" she laughed. "When you watch hotties on the screen, don't you get a sweet tooth?"

I grinned. "Oh, yeah. Come on." I asked her as we laughed down the hall where her stuff was, but saw it all piled up by the door. "Are you expecting an extended stay?"

"It takes hours to look this good, I have you know."

"I believe it." I braced myself as we rounded the kitchen corner. First I brought Eli with his eye piercing and tongue ring, now Ariel…in all her Goth glory. I wondered what Pastor and Mrs. Ruth were going to think.

But as we walked in and Mrs. Ruth looked up, I should have known better. She smiled and asked who my friend was. After introductions with her she asked if we wanted a snack. We said yes, and I tacked on, "Can you make it something sweet?"

Ariel and I both started laughing hysterically. Mrs. Ruth eyed us with parental tolerance as she started to whip up a batch of brownies. So I introduced the kiddos to Ariel.

"Ah!" Hannah gasped. "Just like the mermaid!"

"Oh, yeah. Just like it," Ariel confirmed with a happy grin.

"Do you know Sebastian the crab? Or Cruella?"

"I think Cruella's from the Dalmatian movie, sweetie pie," I told her.

"Or the eels! Were you scared? Did you have to swim away?" Hannah continued.

"Yeah!" Josiah said and grimaced. "Right before she had to kiss Aladdin."

"I think we're mixing up our Disney movies," I said and laughed as they kept going.

"Brownies will be done in about 20 minutes. I can bring them up to you if you want," Mrs. Ruth told us as she wiped Hannah's nose with a tissue. "Are you staying the night Ariel?"

"If that would be ok. My parents are out of town."

"Of course," she answered and smiled at her.

"Mrs. Ruth is like super sweet," Ariel said as we padded back to my room.

"Yeah," I sighed. "They are the two nicest people on the planet."

"So," she drawled out. A pre-emptive to a discussion, no doubt.

"So," I answered back with emphasis.

She shut my door gently and turned to me with a stern face. It was kind of funny really with her nose ring. "I just want to make sure that you're being safe with Eli. Teen pregnancy isn't cool, Clara."

"Isn't cool?" I mocked. "Are you serious?" I whined.

"Totally serious," she said and sat on my bed. "I was a teenager's baby."

"Really?"

"Yes. And my mom has had it rough ever since then. Just please tell me you're being careful."

"I'm a virgin, Ariel," I whispered conspiratorially. "Sealed up like a Swiss bank account."

"Ok, T.M.I."

"Are you?"

"Am I what?" she said and tried to keep a straight face. I gave her a look that said, 'Answer immediately'. "Ok, fine. Yes."

I laughed. "You sound like you're not happy about that."

"Why would I be?" she said, her face twisted like she smelled something bad.

"Uh, because it's a good thing? Why is sex such a big deal? Why do teenagers think that they have to do it? Why does it have to be some huge political statement just because I chose to stay a virgin?"

"Gee. Someone's over thought the subject," she spouted through a giggle and ran a hand over her shorn skull.

"I'm just saying."

"I get it." She smiled at something private as she looked at the wall. "I've had plenty of chances - not that I'm bragging - but I'm just…waiting for something."

"Or someone," I taunted. "Someone whose name rhymes with Matrick?"

She flushed and looked at her boots crossed at her ankles. "No, why?"

"Oh, come on. Girl to girl." I waited for her to look at me. I leaned forward and tried to meet her eyes.

She huffed and then fought a smile, failing. "Oh my gosh, isn't he like the cutest guy you've ever met? Isn't he the sweetest?"

"Yeah," I agreed. "He kind of is."

"But he thinks he's in love with that skank, Sarah." She blanched. "Sorry. I know she was your friend."

"Your actions are what make you." I smiled sadly. "I used to be a *skank*, too."

"Nah," she soothed. "Even I could see that you were trapped."

"Trapped or not, I never even tried to leave." I shook my head. "Let's talk about Patrick some more."

"I thought we agreed we'd call him Matrick."

"If you want to stay in denial you can," I said playfully and sniffed. "Whatever."

But she never laughed at my joke. Her eyes stayed unfocused as she said, "I'm invisible to him."

"No, you're not. You're one of his best friends!" I argued.

"Exactly," she pouted. "The friend zone. He doesn't even see me as a real girl."

"I hate to break it to you, Ariel, but you're kind of hard to miss in the girl department." She looked at me like I was nuts. "You're…" I moved my hands to mirror a girl's body top to bottom, "voluptuous. You've got curves in all the right places."

"I think the nose ring scares people away."

"Yeah," I agreed cautiously. "But the perfect guy for you will look passed all of that and see the you that I see."

She smiled at me and it grew wider before it was a full on grin. "You want to know a secret? A horribly embarrassing and shudder inducing secret?"

"Uh, yeah! Especially after that description."

She took a deep breath and stood. She reached for the nose ring and unconnected it...because it was fake. She pulled the chain from her ear as well and showed me the snaps that made it look so real against her skin. I gave her a questioning look and she shrugged at me. "I'm scared of needles and grubby men poking holes in my body with tattoo sleeved arms, ok? It's completely unacceptable." She sat on the bed and bit her lip. "I'm a fraud."

I laughed. I laughed so hard that I fell to my knees at her feet, holding myself up by gripping her knee. She sulked further. "It's not that funny."

"Ah, Ariel. You're not a fraud."

"I am," she disagreed. "I portray a hard-ace shell on the outside; strong, unapproachable and a rebel. But on the inside, I'm a gooey, emotional, scaredy cat mess."

"I think the whole point of being a rebel is to do what you want. If there were rules for being a rebel, wouldn't that defeat the whole purpose of being a ...rebel?" She looked up at me from under her lashes. "If you want to have a faux piercing, then go for it. I hate needles, too. So what?"

"Really?"

"Yeah. I'm right on this one."

"Honestly," she set the chain on my nightstand and rubbed her nostrils, groaning, "I hate the thing."

"Then why wear it?"

"Because…I only started wearing black to piss off my mom. She wanted me to be this happy, bright girl that had rainbows in her eyes, and when I told her that I wasn't that girl, she pushed and pushed and pushed me. So, I started dressing the exact opposite of the way she wanted. Then everyone at school started calling me a 'Goth', though I never called myself that. It just became expected of me to be this way."

"And the hair?" She looked up again. "It's…pretty short, Ariel."

She cleared her throat. "You want to know another secret?" I nodded. "I have Leukemia. I went into remission last year."

I stilled, my heart slamming to a halt against my ribs. "What?" I whispered.

"I decided to cut my hair off because I knew it was all going to fall out anyway once I started the treatments, right? But it didn't." She scrubbed the short hair with her hand. "I never lost my hair and it was all in vain. I just keep it cut now because like I said, everyone just expects me to be this crazy Goth girl and I don't want it to be said that I caved from peer pressure to be *normal*."

"Wow," I muttered.

"So I get an "A" for shock and awe?" she jested.

"Ariel," I said softly and sat next to her on the bed. Ok, I could do this. I could be the girlfriend. I could be the shoulder to lean on, right? I'd never been those things before with anybody, because my friends were always shallow and didn't care about anyone's problems.

I turned to her and said in a clear voice. "Screw them. Screw them all. Screw anyone that says whether or not you wear your hair a certain way, or dress a certain way, or connect things to your nose or not, or be the product of a teen pregnancy, or be a virgin. Screw them, Ariel! If you want to grow your hair back and wear freaking pastels, you do that and anyone that breathes a word about it doesn't deserve your attention enough to even acknowledge them!"

Her eyes were bugged and had been that way for most of my speech. I worried that I'd gone too far, maybe, but she snatched me to her in a hug. "Wow, Clara. You've got the pep talk thing down."

I laughed and hugged her back. I tried to remember what she looked like when her hair was long, but to be honest - and completely shameful - I couldn't remember. I pulled back to look at her. "Was it too much? I'm kind of new to it."

"It was too much, but that's why I freaking loved it!" She smiled. "Thanks. I don't think I'll let the Goth look go, because it's so easy to shop at Hot Topic and just buy one of everything, but thanks. It's nice to maybe have the option one day."

"Brownies, girls!" Mrs. Ruth called down the hall. "I've decided it's too hazardous to my clean house to leave the munchkins unattended."

I rolled my eyes. "I'll get it."

As I crossed the room, I heard her call my name. "Clara."

"Hmm?" I asked as I turned to look at her.

"Thanks. I mean it."

"No problem." I started walking again, but she's stopped me once more. "Yeah?"

"Don't even think about coming back here without some milk."

I grinned. "Got it."

Four

We watched Vamps hunting Vamps, Vamp hunters and Witches torching Vamps, teenage girls kissing Vamps. And we giggled and swooned through it all. Eventually she passed out, the last half of her fourth brownie still in her hand. I put it aside and pulled the comforter over her. Her pajamas she'd thrown on, after the fastest shower I'd ever seen a girl take, were pink and black bull's-eyes. Her black camisole showed how petite she really was. Though she was curvy, she was slim, too.

I lay down beside her and closed my eyes, ready to see Eli…and there he was. My eyes hadn't been closed for three seconds before Eli was before me on the dock at the quarry. I smiled as I went to him easily and wrapped my arms around his middle.

I thought he'd be eager to pick right back up where we left off, but he accepted me in his arms and rubbed my lower back as he swayed us back and forth. I smiled against his chest. I was still safe in every way with my Eli.

"What's that smile for?" he asked against my forehead. He must have felt my lips move against his chest.

"Nothing, except…everything."

"My beautiful, cryptic Clara." He kissed my forehead.

"I just think it's great that I never have to be anyone but myself with you." I leaned back and looked at him. "But although it's nice to feel safe…intimately…with you, it does make me curious why you don't want to."

His eyebrows lifted, jumping into his hairline almost. "You think I don't want to ravage you right this second?"

I gulped as I felt the crimson rush into my cheeks with lightning speed. "You do?"

"Oh, absolutely," he said low. His eyebrows returned and he watched me as he tortured me with silence and a penetrating stare. "I want to. I just know that you want to wait." He lifted my hand, and in a move that I would have thought was cheesy if I'd seen it from anyone else, he kissed my promise ring. I smiled and watched as his expression changed from one of calm to one of concern…and then to one of happiness.

He wiped under my eye and I balked at the wetness there. He chuckled silently. "You didn't think I was a celibate for any reason other than waiting for you, did you?"

"I don't know. I just thought…I don't know."

"I try to keep myself somewhat…tame around you."

I smoothed my hand over his chest, my fingers catching on the buttons. "Well, you fooled me."

"Mission accomplished." He smiled before taking my hand again. "Come on."

He took me to the end of the dock to an oversized lounge chair with a blanket over the back, and two cans of soda. He helped me into the lounger before climbing in himself and throwing the blanket over us. Then he popped the can open for me and handed it to me. It was still cold.

"Am I really drinking this Dr. Pepper?" I asked as I felt the cold, smooth drink go down my throat. "I mean this is a reverie."

"Reveries are as real as I make them. It's kind of like your real body pauses and waits for you to return, but anything that happens to you in the reverie is real. If you get hurt in one, you'll be hurt in the real world."

"So if I sleep here?"

He looked surprised. "You know, I've never thought about that before." He smiled. "If you sleep in the reverie, your body should be reenergized by it."

"So this whole time you've taken me home in a hurry and we could have just fallen asleep and it would have been the same thing?"

"I guess so. It never crossed my mind before."

"Hmm. The possibilities…" I crooned and set my drink down before snuggling into him. "So this is the plan for tonight?"

His warm fingers played with the strap of my camisole and caressed my shoulder. "Yep. I thought we'd just sit here together," he said softly.

The dock swayed a bit with the gentle waves of the lake under us. There were no waves on a lake at night with no boaters to make them. He must have generated them. Like he generated the moon that was so close and so bright and beautiful, casting a spell over the night all its own.

"This is really beautiful," I whispered.

He pulled my chin up and looked at my face for a few seconds. "Yeah," he breathed, "it is."

He leaned down to kiss me and then pressed my face into his neck. I wiggled my leg in between his and sighed at the comfort I felt. And I fell asleep.

~ ~ ~

"CB, you've got to get up, love," I heard in my ear.

"Mmm, no," I groaned in annoyance.

"Mmm, yes," I heard, followed by a chuckle. "Ariel will be up soon and you need to get back."

Back?

I peeked and saw that it was now daylight in our reverie. And we'd slept - well, I'd slept - on the dock in the chair. Eli had held me all night. I felt the same. I didn't feel tired, but I guessed we'd have to test the sleeping theory when I was in the real world again.

Math was seriously going to suck if I had to go with my body running on no sleep.

"Come on, CB," he coaxed again.

I realized I closed my eyes again and opened them. Eli looked content and I wondered what he did all night. I just lay there like a lump and my leg was still wedged between his, so I know he didn't get up.

"What did you do all night?"

He smiled and ran is hand through my hair. "Watched you," he admitted in a low voice.

"Boring much?" I scoffed.

"Not for me." He had made another sweep through my locks and I fought not to shiver. "It was a new experience. I've never slept with anyone."

"But you don't sleep."

"And I didn't last night either, but I stayed right here while you did. You make all these little noises and sighs..." He smiled again. "You dream, your eyelids move and jump. You..."

"What?" I said, suddenly enraptured with what he was going to say about me when he stopped.

"You said my name," he said with a growly, joyful voice. "A lot."

He covered the blush on my cheeks with his hand and smiled. "I'm sorry," I muttered. "My subconscious is apparently obsessed with you."

He laughed. "I'm totally fine with it, love." He kissed my forehead. "I'm not sure I could be anymore blissful than I am right now."

"Is that something you foreigners say? Love?"

"You foreigners?" he scoffed and laughed. "I've been reduced to a foreigner now?"

"You know what I mean."

"Yes, people overseas say 'love' when they talk to people sometimes. It's a nickname or endearment. But for me, it means something else entirely when I say it to you." He looked at me pointedly. He was asking me silently if I was ready to have the 'I love you' conversation.

I wasn't sure if I was ready to have that conversation or not, but I remembered Ariel waiting for me. "Ariel," I said.

He frowned. "Um…oh, yeah." He cleared his throat. "That girl is causing me problems lately."

"I'm, uh… Thank you for last night. It was a really sweet gesture."

He leaned in and whispered against my mouth, "You're welcome, love."

And then I was on my bed. I opened my eyes to find a freaking-out version of Ariel. She was yelling and then pushing buttons on her phone. I sat up and she screamed like she'd seen a ghost. Then Mrs. Ruth burst through the door yelling for Pastor. She stopped and stared at us.

"What in…the world," she said harshly.

"Sorry," Ariel was saying and hung the phone up and grimaced. "I…she wouldn't…I thought that she was…she wouldn't wake up!"

"I'm awake," I said and smiled. "What's going on?" I tried to play off.

"I've been trying to get you up for like five minutes!" she yelled. "I shook you, I said your name. You were barely breathing!"

"Sleep breathing," I justified. "It slows down when you sleep."

"I slapped you in the face! I thought you died!"

I felt it then, like it was waiting for an explanation to make an appearance. It stung and I groaned as I grabbed my angry cheek. "What the…Ariel!"

"I thought you were in a coma! I called 911!"

"Well, I'm ok," I reasoned and looked at Mrs. Ruth. "I'm ok."

"Are you sure?" she asked and eyed me.

"Yep." I winced at my cheek and glowered at Ariel. "Except my cheek frigging hurts. Thanks, friend."

"You're welcome!" she huffed. "You were about to get mouth to mouth as well. That would have been awesome to wake up to."

I burst out laughing at the scene she created with her words. She followed me and Mrs. Ruth shook her head. I'm sure there was even an eye roll as she turned away.

Once our laughing stopped, she looked at me closely. "I really thought something was wrong with you."

"Sorry. I'm a sound sleeper."

"Apparently. Sorry I slapped you, but it was in the interest of saving lives."

"Forgiven," I said and tried not to wince more. "You shower first."

"Alrighty."

She bounced away with a spring in her step and shut the door. I heard her humming behind the door as she turned on the water. My door opened and Mrs. Ruth came in with a cold Pepsi Max can in hand. "Here, honey."

"Thanks." I started to pop the top, but she stopped me.

"Put that on your cheek first, then you can drink it."

"Ooh, yeah," I grumbled. "Thanks."

After she was gone, it was then that I realized, as I pressed the cold can to my pounding cheek, that I was fully rested. We were right. Sleep in the reverie was just as good as the real thing. I smiled.

When Ariel got out of the bathroom, she had a towel wrapped around her midsection and one around her head. She looked so...normal, for lack of a better word. Without the dark makeup and the piercing and the shaved head, she looked like everyone else.

"I have a favor," she said and chewed on her thumbnail.

"Sure. What's up?"

"Um..." She went to her book bag and pulled out her wallet. "It might be vain to keep this on me, but the day I got the salon to cut off all of my hair, I took a picture." She handed it to me. She was standing in front of the mirror, the reflection of the person taking the picture staring back at her from the side. Ariel looked like someone who was devastated, but trying to be brave.

And holy heart failure, Batman! She was wearing pink.

Her shirt was a pink tank with a yellow one layered underneath. Her long black hair pulled over her shoulder so you could see its length and impressiveness. I remembered her...I never talked to her before, but I remembered this girl.

I looked back up at Ariel. "I'm sorry that I wasn't your friend before."

She shrugged. "It's cool."

"What do you need from me?"

"I want to...be me again." She looked up at the ceiling, like it was hard to talk about. "Like I said, I only went all anti-social and rebel to piss off my parents. They wanted me to work extra hard at being perfect since I was sick. Don't get me wrong," she shook her head, "they're great. But they thought if they just bought me wigs, dressed me in extra expensive clothes, made me feel so super normal," her voice all high and pitchy when she said it, "that I'd forget I had cancer or something. I wanted to brood a little. I wanted to be pissed off a little and I don't think it was asking too much. So I rebelled. What I want is to...wear pink again." Her eyes looked glossy when she said it.

And I understood. Pink didn't mean pink. Pink meant everything that she felt was taken from her when she got cancer. I nodded and grabbed her hand as I made a beeline for my closet. I opened it and dragged her inside.

"Are we going full on or easing into it?"

"Easing," she said as she looked around.

"I'm thinking…these," I said and pulled a pair of black ballet flats from the rack. "No socks or stockings, Ariel. None."

"Ok," she said and gulped.

"And this," I told her as I grabbed a little silver heart necklace from my jewelry box. "And this!" I said excitedly as I reached for a black scarf that had little bits of color to match our uniforms.

"Ok," she repeated.

"Ok," I agreed. "Now my turn."

"What?"

"I want to be more edgy. I've always been this and I want to be something different."

She smiled in tolerance. "You don't have to do this to make me feel better. I made my own decisions. People always stare at me, now they can stare for another reason." She poked at the scarf. "Me in a freaking scarf."

"No, I want to, really. My parents were kind of like yours, I guess. Always wanting me to be perfect, like that solved all high school problems."

"Oh," she blanched, "Clara, I'm so sorry! Here I've been going on about my parents and yours…at least I still have mine. I'm sorry."

"No, it's ok. I need to talk about them. I miss them. Gah, I miss them so much, but they weren't perfect. It makes it easier for me every single time I say their names."

"This'll be a good start," she told me, gripping the items I gave her. "Thank you."

"Not a problem."

We finished getting ready in comfortable, contemplative silence. We both did our makeup in the bathroom at the same time and she didn't put on a smidge of eyeliner, or the nose ring. I on the other hand, put on a bit too much for my usual self, and no lip-gloss or lipstick. We painted each other's fingernails, mine black of course, and hers a pale pink. I was such a poser, but I hoped she understood what I was offering her. As lame as it was, I was hoping that by my causing attention to myself, she wouldn't get so many stares and could make up her mind about what she really wanted to represent.

I slid on her boots. Ah, they weighed a ton each. My socks were up to my calves! She giggled as she slid on the flats I'd given her. She twirled and joked about feeling ten pounds lighter.

"Ha. Try twenty," I groaned as we lugged down the hall.

Five

She laughed differently now, as if some weight was no longer bearing down on her. I smiled at her. Goth was just dandy, but she needed to be who she was and stop hiding to distract others from what was going on. I wondered if anyone at school even knew that she'd been sick.

I knew that Eli would be there to walk us to school once we finished our breakfast, and wasn't surprised a bit when we came outside and found him standing there leaning against the tree in my front yard. He smiled and then cocked his head to the side as we made our way to him.

"Is it opposite day and I didn't get the memo?"

"Nope," I answered and reached up to kiss him. "We're just trying some different things."

"Well," his eyes took me in, toe to head and back again, "you both look very pretty, and I'm not just saying that."

"Thanks, babe," I said. He looked at me as he grabbed my hand and smiled at my endearment.

"Anytime, love."

I bit my lip.

Ariel starting making gagging noises so we both turned to look at her. "Ugh, don't make me barf on my new shoes before we even get to school," she said and laughed as I almost tripped over her ridiculous boots.

"Whoa," Eli spouted as he grabbed my arm, "careful."

"I can't believe you wore these every day, Ariel," I grumbled.

"It takes a learning curve," she replied happily.

As she walked a little ahead of us, Eli leaned over to me. "So, how do you feel this morning?"

"Great. You were right."

He sighed, like he'd been worried about it. "Good. That's good."

We walked, slightly swinging our arms as we crossed the quad at school. I didn't need to go to my locker, so after I waved to Ariel, and gave her a brave smile to encourage her, we went and stood in front of my homeroom. Eli leaned in to me, forcing me to the wall.

"So what's really going on with the getup?" he asked as he eyed my boots once more.

"I just wanted Ariel to feel comfortable. She wanted to try something new...or old, I should say." He frowned, his eyebrow piercing twinkling under the lights of the hall, so I went on. "She hasn't always been like this, but she got sick. Leukemia."

"Oh," he said as if that explained it all. "Well, things like that change people."

"Yeah. So, she wanted to try to be her old self again."

He nodded and said, "And you dressed like this to make her feel more comfortable. I get it." He leaned in and kissed my cheek, speaking his words against my skin. "Wow, that was really sweet of you."

"For a girl who was so self absorbed and concerned about what others thought before, right?" I said begrudged. Eli hadn't said it, but I thought for sure he was thinking it.

"Nope. Just sweet." I sighed and looked around the hall. A few people gave me weird looks or sneers even, but for the most part, no one seemed to care.

"That's the thing about forgiveness...and redemption." His smile said he knew what he was talking about. "What you did before doesn't matter anymore, right?"

He looked at me and waited for me to disagree. If I did, that meant that I thought that all of the things that he'd done - all the things I said didn't matter - that the forgiveness was moot.

"It's not moot," I muttered.

"What?"

I grabbed his face in between my hands. "It's not moot!"

He smiled, while bunching his brow in confusion. "All right. It's not moot."

"You're right. Thank you."

"Ok," he agreed reluctantly and let me pull him to me. I kissed him like the sun would boil us into oblivion as any moment. I kissed him as if this was my final breath. I felt his hands slam into the wall behind us to keep us from falling as I breathed him in deep, and when I pulled away he stood with a stunned and all too familiar needful expression on his face.

I let his face go from between my hands and wanted to smile as I turned for my class, but instead just watched him watch me as I slid into my classroom, leaving him in a stunned stupor in the hall.

I giggled silently all the way to my seat.

~ ~ ~

I met Ariel at her locker before lunch. She was anxious and fidgeting with the buttons of her vest as she stared into her locker. I waved a hand in front of her face and she jumped and squeaked.

"Oh, sorry," she said.

"What's up with you?"

"Nothing," she answered too quickly.

"Nothing, huh?" I muttered and fit the pieces together in my mind. It was right before lunch and Ariel had no classes with Patrick. This was the only time of day she saw him. "I'm calling bullcrap on that one."

She sighed in defeat and said, "It's stupid that I care so much what he thinks." She looked at me. "He barely knows I exist outside of our group."

"That's not true. You're friends. He'll notice this. I guarantee it."

"Ok, come on. I'm starving and it's better to get it over with. Just like a band-aid."

I linked my arm with hers and practically dragged my feet in the massive boots to the cafeteria. I figured Eli would be waiting there for me, but Ariel needed someone right now. And if Patrick pulled the idiot card and made her cry with his lack of noticing, I'd hurt him. Or get Eli to, whichever.

"Ok, big moment," she breathed as we rounded the last corner and then shook her head. "It's not even that big of a change. It's not a big deal."

"You're fine on many levels," I joked. "Smokin'."

She laughed. "Thanks."

Eli was waiting and smiled at us when he saw us coming. "Hey."

"Hey, you," I replied and grinned as I walked passed him.

He chuckled behind us and jogged to catch up. I linked my arm with his, too. "Are we off to see the wizard?"

Ariel and I laughed, catching the attention of the lunchroom who watched us. I was tempted to flip them off, but knew my mother looking down on me would not approve. I pulled Ariel to our table first and set our stuff down. Eli put his hands on my hips from behind to guide me to the lunch line, as was customary, and we began to make our way. But I heard Ariel's groan beside me.

We turned to see Patrick walking in with Sarah. She was trying to stifle a giggle and he was hiding a smile. She winked as she walked away to her table and he came to ours, but not before one last glance. That glance was the final twist in the knife for Ariel.

She started to bolt, but he was blocking the way in between the tables and there was nowhere else to go. He smiled as he came and then slowed his advance. "Whoa. Looky here."

"Shut up," she muttered. I could tell all of the charisma and confidence she had two seconds ago had been sucked out of the room, just like that.

"She's totally hot, right?" I asked him and went to her side, linking my arm through hers. "I can't wait for your hair to grow out."

"You're growing your hair out? Why?" he asked and then looked at me. "And why are you dressed like that?" He seemed almost angry. I was confused. Ariel shied away from him into my side. "Answer me, Ariel," he said softly. "Why are you dressed like that? Clara shouldn't have made you feel like you weren't good enough." He eyed me. "That was a really crappy thing to do, Hopkins."

"This was my decision," she cut in. "I wanted to be the old me again."

"The old you? There's only ever been *you*. You never changed. Maybe your clothes did, but you never did."

I realized they'd been friends for a long time then. I wondered if he knew about her being sick.

"I was different," she argued. "I was completely different. I want to be that girl again. The girl who could wear whatever she wanted and it didn't matter. She was pretty and happy and…"

He glared at me once more. "What did you say to her? I know she slept over last night. What did you do?"

"Nothing!" she shrieked at him. "She didn't tell me anything. I can make up my own mind, you know."

He eyed her shoes. "So why did you decide to go all *cool table* on us then?"

"Ahg! I'm so done." She stomped off and it was my turn to glare at Pat.

"What?" he defended. "I was trying to help her see that she didn't need to wear your stupid shoes to fit in."

"She's not trying to fit in, you idiot," I chastised softy. "She's trying to remember who she was before she got sick."

"Got sick? She got sick at your house last night?"

He didn't know... Yikes. That's a big cat to let out of the bag. I looked away, but still saw his wheels turning.

He cursed. "I knew something was going on. I knew it. She always said it wasn't, but..."

"She's in remission," I offered.

"So the whole...piercings and hair and clothes was to hide her being sick?" I nodded. "And she wants to go back to being *normal* again because that's really what she was all along and this was just a front," he said, not phrasing it as a question because it no longer was.

I nodded again."Yep."

"But why was she so scared then? She looked like she was about to throw up. That's why I thought you were pushing her into it. If she was really wanting to change, she wouldn't be so upset-"

"Idiot!" I said again and laughed. "You're such a guy."

He took a deep breath and stuck his hands into his pockets. Then it hit him and I saw it take him over. He grimaced and then looked at me in question. I nodded. "Yes, Pat. You're a jackass."

"I *am* a jackass." He rubbed his head. "I always wondered. I mean...we both had a crush on each other and went on a couple of dates and then she just stopped...being interested. Oh, crap." He grabbed his head. "That's when she got sick! That's when she cut her hair and missed so much school and I thought she was just over me, like I was a phase." He shook his head. "I thought she wanted to just be friends. Ah, man. I'm such a jackass."

"We've established that, Pat." I grinned. "Now put some feet to the pavement."

He took off after her. Our other lunch buddies came and asked what was going on. I just waved them off and dragged Eli to the lunch line. It was pizza day, so I resorted to the salad bar.

It was when we were laughing about something later that I felt hands on my shoulders. Eli was sitting next to me, so it could only be one other person. "Tate, don't-" I started, but when I turned it wasn't Tate I saw, it was Finn…and Enoch was standing by the door.

"Hello again, lovely," he sneered at me and then looked at Eli, who was stunned silent, but still wrapping his arm around me in protection as he stared at him. "Come with us outside and nothing happens to the feelers. Just you though. The girl stays."

Six

"Finn, what are you doing?" Eli asked him.

"Saving your life."

Eli scoffed, but gulped as we stood and he pulled me behind him. "What's this about?"

"Hey," Dee interrupted. "Who's this?" she asked of Finn. No one answered her and she huffed. "Well? New guy? What's your name?"

"My name's *get lost,*" he spouted.

She shrieked and Tate wasn't far behind. "What's going on?" He looked at me. "You ok? What's going on, Clara?"

"Nothing for you to worry about, buddy," Finn said and patted Tate on the arm. "Now run along."

"Watch it, *buddy,*" Tate sneered. "Eli, this a friend of yours?"

"I'd use that term loosely."

"Come on, Clara." Tate held his hand out for me. "Let them settle whatever this is."

"Nope," I said, shaking my head. Tate still thought that after everything he could come over and order me around and I'd just go with him like a scared little girl. "I'm not leaving."

Tate's jaw tightened. "Don't be stupid, Clara. Come with me. Now."

Eli turned to him, but before anything could be done, Finn punched Tate in the jaw, letting him fall to the floor like a lump. Finn growled, "Outside."

"I'm not leaving Clara."

Finn laughed and ticked his head toward the door. "Enoch is coming with us. But it wouldn't matter, now would it? Since she's bound the Thames family to her like the evil succubus she is."

"Don't," Eli hummed low and inched closer to Finn. "Don't, Finn."

"Why not?" he laughed and got right in Eli's face. "That's what she is." He looked at me over Eli's shoulder, but Eli grabbed him by the collar.

"Don't even look at her if you're going to call her that."

Everybody else was looking at me though. They were looking at all of us and the spectacle we were making, though no one seemed too worried about Tate. I pulled gently on the back of Eli's shirt to let him in on it. He understood and eased his hands away from Finn's neck. "Let's take it outside-"

"That's what I wanted in the first place!" Finn yelled.

"-but I'm not leaving Clara."

Finn pushed away from Eli and huffed. "Whatever, Elijah."

"Don't call me that," Eli muttered and grabbed my bag from the table in one hand and my hand in the other. Finn was way ahead of us as he scooted down the hall, pausing a fraction of a second before leaving through the school front doors.

I was afraid to ask what was going on. He said Finn had been a friend of sorts, but that little encounter just now looked anything but friendly. We were almost to the doors when I saw it. That was what Finn had paused for; he felt their lust, passion, whatever.

Because outside of my math classroom, Patrick and Ariel were kissing in the most tender, sweet way I'd ever seen anyone kiss. She was leaning against the wall, he was leaning into her with a hand on her jaw as he kissed her. They didn't look up or even notice us as we followed Finn out the door. My joy for them was short lived as my own fear spiked when I saw Finn and Enoch leaning against the tree in the quad.

Finn took a deep breath to acknowledge my fear, but Enoch, being who he was, licked his lips and grinned. It made me even more scared that he looked so happy about what they had to tell us and I knew it was nothing good.

Eli picked up my fear then, which meant it was pretty intense. He sucked in a breath and leaned into my ear. "Don't be scared. I'm right here."

I nodded, but agreeing didn't make my fear go away.

Eli got right down to business. "What?

Enoch answered first. "The jig's up. The Horde is coming back and this time, they won't be pussy footing around."

"We've been hearing some things at the Consumed Clubs," Finn said.

"So, you two are buddies now, huh?" Eli asked and cocked his pierced brow.

"I went and found him," Enoch said. "I thought Finn could convince you to get rid of this…this…" he eyed our wrists with distain, "bond before anyone else could. That you'd listen to him and know that all this is going to do, brother, is cause problems for you and her. Don't you see that?"

"Touching," Eli rebutted. "Since when do you care?"

"Since she was attached to my bloody wrist!"

Eli looked down at me and then back at them. "You wasted a trip. We'll deal with the Horde."

"Eli, come on, man," Finn reasoned. "You can't win this."

"So your suggestion is what? Kill her?" Eli yelled.

"Hey!" I defended.

"Take her to The Wall and get it reversed!" Finn yelled back.

"No! Even if there was a way to reverse it, which there isn't, I wouldn't! You and Enoch don't get it. She didn't trap me into this. I…" He looked back at me and I knew what he had been going to say. "I'm…happy right where I am," he said instead.

"As someone who was trapped by a succubus would say," Finn spouted sarcastically.

"Enough! I'm not having this conversation." Eli started to pull me away from them, but Finn stopped him.

"The Horde is planning retribution for you."

Eli stopped, but didn't turn. "Well…they'll have to catch me first."

"You have to leave," Enoch spouted gruffly. "And yes, this is the bond talking. Even if I'm not here, it's constantly on my mind that you're here and she's possibly in danger. That's why I went to Finn; to talk some sense into you!"

"We'll leave," Eli conceded. "We've been prepared for this to happen." He turned to look at him. "So I'm to believe you both just came here to talk sense into me?"

"I've always been soft," Finn said and laughed humorlessly. "Soft is good to get what I want from the feelers, but what you are is...I'm Charmin, you're a frigging down feather pillow, Eli! Too soft, man, and it's gonna get you strung up to a tree and branded."

"Again?" Eli growled.

Finn pulled on his hair. "Geez, Eli." It sounded like an apology, but I was sure that was about as apologetic as a Devourer got.

"We're out of here tonight," Eli told them. "Happy?"

"Is this thing still around my wrist?" Enoch asked rhetorically. "Then I'm not happy."

Eli turned without another word and took me across the street to my house. I knew exactly what he was doing and I just let him do it. We went straight down the hall to my room and he threw my backpack on the bed, dumping out everything. I just watched him as he went to my dresser and grabbed two pairs of jeans and a few shirts, throwing them inside the bag.

When he opened my top drawer, I opened my mouth to protest, but nothing came out. He grabbed a handful of my underwear without really looking at them and stuffed them into the bag, only barely glancing at me.

"Toothbrush, Clara," he commanded softly.

I obeyed in a daze. I was about to get my wish. I was leaving this town, albeit not the way I had imagined. But I was leaving and there was something thrilling in that even though my life was in danger. But it also made me feel guilty in a way I never had before. That Finn guy was right. Eli was tied to me because I had bound us and I slowed him down, put him in danger, and forced him to look after me. A wretched balloon of regret began to bloom in my chest.

I brought him my toothbrush and a tube of toothpaste, along with my small makeup bag from the bathroom. He stuffed all that into the bag and then took my hand again to lead me down the hall. He stopped and hovered outside the kitchen. Mrs. Ruth was chopping something. The babies must've been down for a nap because the house was quiet.

He looked back at me as if asking for permission. My mind ran. What was I going to tell Pastor and Mrs. Ruth? Then I saw the way he was looking at me; a shameful way. I knew then what he wanted.

"It's ok, Eli. It'll be easier on them if you persuade them to let me go."

"But I hate it," he admitted and sagged even more. "I hate it so much for you to see me like that."

"I'm sorry. I can talk them into it," I suggested and rubbed his arm. "We never really discussed what I was going to do after graduation, but they had to know it wasn't going to be forever, right?"

"I hate it, Clara, but it has to be done." He kissed my forehead. "And the fact that I'd do anything for you is there, too. Just stay here, ok?"

I nodded and leaned on the wall as I heard a surprised Mrs. Ruth say hello to Eli. I heard him murmuring and her agreeing. About a minute and a half later, he came around the corner and grabbed my hand.

We made a swift getaway from my house. I didn't ask him what was said. It was obvious he didn't want to talk about it. I'd ask him later. We passed the bird on the way to his bedroom. He started packing up some of his stuff as well.

"I only have four thousand in emergency cash," he explained. "We'll buy whatever we need, but we need to lay low for a while and not use any bank cards or anything. The cash needs to last for as long as possible."

"I wish I could help in that department."

He shook his head at me. "That's not what I meant."

"I know, but my parents didn't have life insurance. It was just one of those things that didn't get done before they died. So we lost the house and everything. My sister and I split the money from all the stuff in the house that got sold, but it was only a couple thousand dollars. I've blown through that on school stuff."

"I'm sorry," he said as he took his uniform shirt off and threw on a Ramones t-shirt over his wife beater. "That sucks, CB."

"Hey, how come you got to change out of your uniform?"

"Because I don't look as cute as you do in it." He smiled. "You mind going to the kitchen and grabbing something to snack on? Just in case we can't get something tonight."

"Sure. I can play domesticated housewife for a few minutes."

He grinned wider. "Thank you, darling," he said all husband like.

"I could get used to that," I muttered to myself.

"What was that?"

"Nothing, darling!" I yelled back. I heard him chuckling as I went. I passed the bird, who stayed silent, but watchful, as I made my way through the living room. I'd never been in his kitchen before, but it was pretty much in the same spot in every house, right?

And boy was it huge! I searched the cabinets and found them stocked with chips, granola bars, pop tarts, cereal and beef jerky. Beef jerky? I grabbed the box of Cinnamon Toast Crunch, the granola bars box, a couple bottles of water from the counter and went back down into Eli's basement.

I almost stumbled on the stairs, my legs seeming to go numb out of nowhere. I shook my leg and then my head to clear it. Weird.

"Why do you have so much food?" I asked when I hit the last step. "I know you like to eat, but some of that is definitely chick food."

"Well, I thought you might start hanging out over here more," he said quietly as he tied his boot strings. He was now in jeans, boots and a grey Ramones t-shirt that was a little tight on his arms. He looked up at me as he finished.

"Really?" I asked.

"Yeah."

"That's really sweet," I said as I put my plunders in the bag with my clothes. I turned to him, but he was right up against me. "Really sweet."

"The fact that I have a strange hankering for beef jerky had no affect on the decision, though."

I laughed. "I'm sure."

He wrapped his arms around me, burying his face in my neck. "Are you sure this is ok?" he said, suddenly serious.

"We have to go," I said. "We knew they'd come back. It was just wishful thinking to think we could stay here until graduation."

He pulled back to look at me. "I can't believe how cavalier you're being about this. You pitched a fit - a fit, I remind you - about us staying until graduation. Remember?"

"That was before." I looked away.

"Before what?" he said and maneuvered to catch my eye. "Before what, Clara?"

"Before I realized that even though you can't be killed, that doesn't mean that you can't suffer." I put my hand over the spot on his heart, the raised circle from the brand where his parents had him tortured. "They can still hurt you and it was selfish of me to tell you we had to stay." I sighed and let him see all the emotion in me and feel it, too, if he wanted to. "I did this to you. I," I grabbed his wrist, "put this on you, like some leash. You couldn't leave me if you wanted to. So to tell you that we have to stay here is pretty darn selfish when I've really given you no choice in the matter."

"You can't really think that," he said incredulously. "Is this because of what Finn said?"

"No, it's because it's the truth."

He sighed and watched me. "This is where the leading lady tries to save the guy from himself. He is willing to give up everything for her and she, in her misguided attempt to save him, tells him that she's at fault for all of their troubles and he has to beg her to realize that's not true. That the guy wants to be bound to her more than he's ever wanted anything his whole life. That she saved him that day, not condemned him, and he has to convince her that his love is real and that he is sound of mind."

I bit my lip to stop the smile as he spouted my speech back at me. I'd said that almost verbatim to him not a few days ago when he said he should never have let me stay with him. That he should leave or...something. He was right.

Technically, Eli could leave, couldn't he? And he stayed…he stayed through all of my drama with Tate. He stayed for me.

I pulled him to me and hugged his midsection, which was quickly becoming my favorite part of him. It was strong, but gentle. Always right there within reach, protecting me, guarding me, warm, loving, open arms and comfort. He pressed his lips to my forehead and hugged me to him. "No more talk of leaving or regrets. Do you hear me, Clara Belle Hopkins?"

"Mmhmm. I hear you," I sighed. "I just…"

Gah!! 'I love you' was on the tip of my tongue every second! It was bursting to come out. I bit my lip again, locking it inside.

"I just…too," he said and smiled. "So much, Clara."

That was as close as we'd ever been to saying it and it made my heart beat hard in my chest. He picked up on my happiness immediately and groaned against my hair as he hugged me tighter. I smiled my secret smile. I was the only one who could ever give him this again. I was the only one who could give him what he needed, or make him feel. He really was mine.

"We better go," I said, but he held me tighter.

"Just wait another minute," he said gruffly. "I just need to feel you for another minute."

So I let everything go. I wished in that moment that I knew what love *felt* like. Eli was feeling my love for him right now, and I wondered what it actually felt like, to not just be told, but to know, without a shadow of doubt because you could literally feel it.

After a few minutes he took a deep breath and leaned my head back. He kissed my lips once and then got our bags, taking them to the living room upstairs.

The bird took that moment as we were passing to go into a fit. He squawked and screeched. I covered my ears it was so loud and Eli dropped our bags to the floor. He looked at the bird and tapped the cage with his finger. "What is wrong with you?"

The bird answered, "A Goblin's tooth is all you need."

We looked at each other. What? What did that mean?

"A Goblin's tooth?" Eli asked it.

"A Goblin's tooth is all you need," Cavuto repeated.

Eli sighed and lifted his hands in a 'whatever' motion. He opened the bird's cage and held out a smaller one with a handle. The bird went right into it. Crap. We had to take the bird with us.

When Eli walked passed his car, I stopped. "We aren't taking your car?"

He shook his head. "We can't. We need to be inconspicuous and my car is definitely not that."

"So what is inconspicuous then?"

He smirked and jerked his head for me to follow him. We walked a few blocks before I got the drift. "A train? We're taking the train? To where?"

He set the bird down and opened his wallet at the window. "Right now? We're just getting out of here. We'll figure it out later." He looked at the attendant. "Two and a bird for...Colorado."

"Actually," we heard behind us, "four and a bird for New Mexico."

We looked back to see Finn smiling and Enoch looking around with disdain.

"What are you doing?" Eli asked him.

"Saving you," Finn said sarcastically. "We're going to The Wall."

"I don't need to go to The Wall," Eli argued. "I already told you-"

"But you didn't consider that maybe there's something you could gain from The Wall yourself." He smiled and looked at me. "What do you say, human? Want to see if there's a way to live forever?"

"What?"

"You're human. You'll die one day. Maybe we can work together to get to The Wall and see if someone there can help you."

"So..." I thought. "You want to go to The Wall to see if you can have me unbound from Eli, but you want me to think I'm going to The Wall to see about turning myself immortal."

"Now you're getting it. A common journey, no matter the outcome."

"What's The Wall?" I asked Eli.

"It's a meeting place for supernaturals." He glared at Finn. "A dangerous place where very few humans go."

"Maybe there's some magical thing that can be done to stop the Horde?" I offered. "I don't know, but Enoch has to keep me safe and Finn, whatever his ulterior motive, wants to keep *you* safe. So it might not be a bad idea to let them tag along. I do want to find out...some things."

Enoch scoffed, "As far as I'm concerned, you're tagging along with us."

"Whatever," I disregarded. I heard him snort from behind me. "What do you think, Eli?"

"I think Finn convinced you that going to The Wall is a good idea and that you can find a fairy who'll grant you forever-life in a bottle." He sighed and held my face in his hands. "It just doesn't work that way."

"I have no idea how it works, but I'm in your life now, right? It wouldn't hurt to show me the ins and outs of your world. If for no other reason that I know who and what to trust."

"Trust no one, Clara. Trust no one or nothing but me." He sighed and looked back to the attendant. "Four and a bird for New Mexico, please."

Seven

"Gloating doesn't look good on you, Finn," Eli said from our seats.

"I have it on good authority that it does," he said with a smirk.

We were sitting across from a smug Finn and a pissed Enoch who couldn't be pleased no matter what you did. The train seats were two by two facing each other so we had some semblance of privacy.

Our bags were snuggly pressed into the overhead bin. I say ours as in Eli's and mine because Finn or Enoch brought nothing with them. I never saw Enoch with anything anyway. The bird was in another car with our other bag.

"Hungry?" Eli asked me as he turned from Finn. "You didn't eat much lunch today."

"I am actually. I brought," I reached up and grabbed my bag down, "cereal."

"Of all the food in my cabinets you brought cereal to eat dry?" he said amusedly.

"Yep," I grinned as I opened the seal. A waft of fresh cinnamon hit me and I groaned as I popped a few in my mouth.

Eli laughed and reached into the box to get a few himself. Our crunching couldn't be heard over the train's loud screeching and rumbling as it blared down the tracks. It had only been about twenty minutes since we left the station and we had a butt load of miles left to go.

I texted Ariel and told her I'd be out of town with Eli for a few days. She balked as much as one can through text and told me I was crazy. Missing school and going on strange, sporadic vacations with my boyfriend was out of character for me. Yeah, didn't I know it? But she kind of refuted all the maternal advice when she asked for details as soon as I returned. I smiled as I agreed.

After a while, I began to drift off. Eli pulled the armrest up from between us and leaned me to lay my head on his lap. He stretched out, crossing his ankles, and I didn't fight him as he leaned down and whispered in my ear, "Go to sleep, love."

With one of his hands in my hair and the other on my back, I plummeted into sleep.

~ ~ ~

I woke to voices. Heated, straining, upset voices. I didn't open my eyes, I just waited to see what was happening.

"Yes, that's the only reason I'm helping you. I'm hoping that once we get there, and the bond is removed, that you'll be your old self again and the girl can be sent packing."

"And I told you," Eli argued back to Finn in a hiss, "that I'm not some ensnared animal. I chose her as my mate first. I'm not the same person I was forty five years ago when we plundered the clubs of Los Angeles!" He sighed. "I never understood why you were a little different from other Devourers, I still don't, but I accepted you as you were. You don't have to like it, but I'm asking you to do the same for me right now. I am not the same person anymore and won't be ever again, no matter what scheme you come up with. I changed before I even met this girl. You just weren't around to see it."

"But I heard all about it," Finn rebutted and then stayed strangely quiet.

"Angelina," Eli guessed and laughed under his breath. "So are you going to finally admit it?"

Finn hesitated before saying, "You never wanted her."

"Absolutely right, I didn't. I still don't and never will. Have at it."

"That's such bullcrap, Elijah! You were set to take over everything. Why did you have to be so stupid?"

"I didn't want it," Eli growled, his grip on my arm tightening just a tad. "I didn't want any of it. And the only reason Angelina ever wanted me was so she could claim my family's fortune."

"You never wanted her? Really? The most perfectly proportioned woman made on this earth and below it wants you to be her one and only, and you want nothing to do with it?"

"You've got it. It had nothing to do with my parents. They didn't betray me until I ran. And I was running away from her, so shut up, Finn. I'm not joking. If you came to just talk me into going to Angelina you can just jump off now. As far as I know Angelina is in Resting Place with the Goblins anyway. Besides, I never was one for your sloppy seconds."

"You're such a bastard." I heard a scuffle of feet as he stood from his seat. "She only came to me because she missed you."

"Missed me?" Eli laughed humorlessly. "She never *had me* to miss me. And this is one of those times when you being soft really pisses me off, Finn. She used you and you know it. You need to just admit it to yourself so you can stop being obsessed with her."

"I knew she was using me to get to you, I just didn't care. She was a hot piece-"

"Don't. Care."

"Whatever. I can't wait until we get there and some grimy Witch lets us know that you can take that bond off of your wrist. Then you'll stop being such a pansy and start being the Elijah I always knew."

"That Elijah is gone," Eli said sternly. "Eli is all that's left."

I heard steps leaving. I kept my eyes shut, feeling Eli's hands smoothing and soothing me. He didn't seem upset by his talk with Finn. In fact, he seemed completely at ease. He even started to hum the words softly to Coldplay again, *Green Eyes* this time, as he ran his fingers through my hair.

Honey, you should know,

that I could never go on without you.

Green eyes

Honey, you are the sea

upon which I flow.

And I came here to talk

I think you should know.

Green eyes

you're the one that I wanted to find.

And anyone who tried to deny you,

must be out of their minds.

'Cause I came here with a load

and it feels so much lighter since I met you.

I just sat and listened to him, soaking him and his contentment into myself. I thought I was about to get hurt when they started talking about Angelina. I thought Eli was about to turn on the jealousy over Finn and her, but he wasn't jealous. He wasn't even angry.

I chastised myself once again for doubting him. He always pulled through for me, always ready to take whatever I dished, always willing to risk everything for me. Finn and Enoch were on this very train because Eli was trying to please me.

Enoch? Where was he? I peeked my eyes open and saw the seats across from us were empty. The train's lights were off and soft snores could barely be heard around us.

I sat up, suddenly apparently, as Eli jumped in surprise.

"Hey," he said and smiled. "Did you sleep well? You've been out for a few hours."

"Where's everyone?"

He shrugged. "Who cares? You want something? I can go and get you a soda from the machine-"

I ended his sweet announcement with a swift kiss. I climbed over onto his lap. It was the very first time I'd ever been in a guy's lap where I hadn't been put there by grabby hands. Eli huffed a surprised breath against my lips and laughed nervously as I wrapped my arms around his neck and kissed him like there was no one else there.

There was, though. There was a frigging train full of people, but it was dark and everyone was asleep.

His hands rested hesitantly on my sides as if he wasn't sure if I was even awake and knew what I was doing. I pushed one of his hands down to my hip, and brought the other up my cheek. That seemed to be a signal for him. The hand on my hip gripped and pulled as the one on my cheek caressed and made me feel infinitely loved and looked after.

And safe.

And his tongue was an entity all its own. I swear, once I opened my mouth to his, it was like another world was waiting there. He took over and gave me every kind of shiver, goose bump and moan I could imagine myself doing. When he pressed a finger to my lips, I realized he was telling me that I had to be quiet.

I nodded my agreement and he grinned, the moonlight from our window barely enough to see him, before he pulled me back to him and devoured me in the moonlight.

I felt myself shift; my beliefs and non-beliefs and comfort levels crashing down. What wasn't acceptable to me before was becoming something not only acceptable, but something I wanted. I let it all go and just felt everything. He sucked in that telling breath that told me I was giving him what he needed. Then he groaned against my mouth and pulled back. He touched my lips again, with his thumb this time, and smiled as he said breathlessly, "We've got to stop."

"I'll be quiet," I promised in a sultry whisper before kissing his neck. He groaned again and pulled back once more.

"You can, but I can't." He leaned in to whisper in my ear, "Do you have any idea what your tongue is doing to me?" I smiled slightly and waited for us both to catch our breath.

I was disappointed that we had to stop, but it could only go so far on a train anyway, right?

"What did I do to deserve that?" he asked as he leaned back and rubbed my arms.

"Nothing," I said, the grin unstoppable.

He thought with a frown and then smiled as if he understood. "Ah, you were awake and listening, weren't you? You little sneak."

"I love your accent when you say 'little'."

He leaned forward and pressed his lips to my ear. "Little." I groaned and giggled as he held me to him. "Are you satisfied that Angelina is history?" I nodded and felt him breathe deeply from my neck. "Good."

He leaned his seat back to recline a little. I thought that maybe I should get back into my seat, but he pulled me to lie on his chest. I sighed and rubbed the promise ring on my finger. It seemed to all be falling into place the way my mom always wanted for me. I smiled hugely against his shirt when Eli pushed my fingers away and took over the rubbing, like he understood that the meaning behind it, not just the ring itself, was precious and important to me.

"Thank you."

He lifted his head a bit. "For what, love?"

"For being exactly what I was looking for."

He sighed and kissed the top of my head. "You couldn't ever say anything better than that to me. Thank you, sweetheart."

I went back to sleep with his soft humming in my ear and his hands on me making me warm, safe and secure.

Eight

It was dark still. My head pounded behind my eyes and I was freezing. I opened my eyes to find I was alone in the train seat. I looked around, but saw no one. Not even any other passengers. I stood and peered over the seats, but saw no one. Hmmm.

I looked out the window and saw a red light way off in the distance. I squinted to see it as it got closer, my breath fogging up the glass. It was actually two red lights and they were moving quickly.

Eyes. They were eyes and the person careening towards me wasn't human. Angelina was laughing and her wild hair blew behind her. She stopped at the glass even as the train lurched on. She stared at me and I stared back in fright. She licked her lips and smiled before scratching her nails on the window. It began to crack with the movement of her nails and I tried to turn, but my feet seemed glued to the spot.

The window began to rattle and shake. Then it shattered, the glass blowing and cutting into my skin. I screamed in fright, but felt no pain. Then Eli's arms were around me and I felt really warm.

I opened my eyes again to find it was morning. The train was still moving, the sun peeking out over the horizon. Eli still had me on his lap and was looking at me strangely. I looked over to see our few neighbors looking around their seats curiously.

A quick look back at Enoch and Finn put my fear to realization as they both looked at me as if I were an idiot. Eli pulled me back to look at him. "Are you ok? You were just dreaming."

"I'm ok." I looked at the other train goers. "I'm fine. Thank you for your concern," I said sarcastically when they all just kept staring.

"You're sure?" Eli held my face in his hands. "You screamed."

"It was a bad dream, like you said. Angelina…well, she wasn't being nice."

"Angelina is gone, love," he said. "I have no doubts that she is as dead as a Devourer can get."

"I know." I took a deep breath. "I'm sorry."

He scoffed. "Are you kidding? Come on. Let's get some breakfast from the Café car."

"Please."

He gripped my hand as he shielded me from eyes that looked at me with pity, as if I had something wrong with me. I glowered at them making them turn away. We had to go down a couple of cars before we reached the one with food. And when he opened the pressure door, the smell of coffee hit me. I groaned aloud and Eli looked back at me, a chuckle on his lips as he led the way to the bar.

"What'll it be folks?" the guy asked, his crisp bowtie and white shirt ridiculous.

"Coffee first," Eli said, hooking an arm around my waist. "We'll go from there."

"You got it."

"What'll it be, love?" He placed a menu in front of me.

"Wow," I said and I scanned the pages. "They've got everything. What are you having?"

"A pile of pancakes."

"That sounds good," I agreed as I closed the menu and accepted the coffee from across the bar. I sipped it and didn't even care that it burned as it went down. It was hot and strong.

Eli told the man what we wanted and he instructed us to find a seat. We did and waited. Eli asked me if I wanted to talk about my dream. I said I didn't. My head still hurt though; the same pounding behind my eyes as in the dream.

I rubbed them with my fingers and Eli sat in the booth next to me. "What's up?"

"Just a headache."

"Must be a bad one. You're pretty pale all of a sudden, Clara." He felt my forehead and it stung for him to touch me. I hissed. He jerked his hand back and eyed me with a clinical eye. "What's going on?"

"I don't know. It just hurts." I tried to smile reassuringly. "I'll be fine, babe."

"Here we go," the waitress said as she gave us our plates. "Matching orders. How cute."

I could barely muster a smile, let alone manage friendly banter. Eli took care of that for me though and carried on a light conversation with the older lady as I dug into my flapjacks. I closed my eyes trying to ease the headache away. Then I felt a tap on my shoulder. I looked up to see the waitress holding out her hand.

I put my hand under hers and she dropped a small packet of Excedrin Migraine into my palm. "Your boyfriend said you could use these. Drink lots of water with them."

"Thank you." I opened the packet quickly and downed the pills. When I glanced back at Eli, he hadn't even taken a bite. "Eat, you. I'm fine."

"You eat," he rebutted. "I'm worried about you." He pushed my hair back behind my ear. "Not to sound like a jerk, but you don't look so good."

"I don't feel good, either." My stomach groaned, and not in a good way. "Ugh. I'm not even sure I can eat this," I said as I sat back. "You eat."

"I don't have to eat to survive, remember? I only came here for you, and if you're done, then so am I. Come on." He pulled me from the booth, lifting my cup of coffee to take with us, and throwing a few bills on the table.

"You look right peeked, honey," our waitress said as Eli wrapped an arm around my waist. I wanted to resort to sarcasm at her comment. Something like, 'Thank you, Captain Obvious', but refrained. I was very strange feeling in the emotional department, as well as the physical.

"Clara," I heard loudly in my ear and recoiled.

"What?" I said in irritation. "Why are you yelling?"

Eli tipped my chin up and looked at my face closely. I looked around the room without moving my head. We were no longer in the Café car. We were in a bathroom. I looked back up at him in question. I didn't even remember him bringing me there. "What's going on? Why were you yelling?"

He held my face gently and looked into my eyes. He looked upset, but wouldn't answer me. I just watched him. His face seemed to swim, as if I were drugged or something. I squinted to make it go away. He moved his thumb over my cheek before saying, "What is going on with you?"

But he wasn't talking to me, he was talking *about* me.

"What's wrong, Eli?"

"I don't know, baby." He pulled me to him, wrapping me in the warm cocoon of his arms."You're scaring me though."

He sounded scared, too. I gripped him tightly. "I'm sorry."

He laughed and pulled back to let his forehead touch mine. "Only you would apologize for something like that."

"What's the matter? How did we get in here?"

He gulped. "You don't remember?" I shook my head 'no'. "You…passed out in the Café car. I picked you up and brought you in here and tried to wake you up."

"Why would I pass out?"

"I don't know," he hedged, too carefully. "But your eyes…"

"What?" I asked. I could have just turned to look in the mirror myself, but the way he was speaking scared me more than anything. I let him tell me instead.

"Your eyes are purple."

The gasp hung in my throat. "But I thought you said they'd be green, that they couldn't be purple."

"They can't," he whispered. "They can't, Clara." He gulped again and brushed a thumb across my lips. "It's a good thing we're headed to The Wall, because I have to figure out what's going on with you. Someone there can help, though it'll come with a price."

I turned to the mirror slowly. The purple in Eli's eyes looked natural and sexy. The purple in my eyes made me look sick. Creepily pale and sick. I turned away from the mirror.

"Eli… I'm…" I felt myself begin to shake. I felt wrong and Eli could tell that.

"You're scared, I know." He licked his bottom lip and grimaced. "Gah, I hate the taste of your fear."

I let him lift me. I wrapped my arms around his neck and my legs around his waist. He held me easily and pressed me to him. Before I knew it we were back in our seats, but he didn't put me down. He reclined the seat once more and sat down with me in his lap. He lifted my face with his finger and looked at me, almost sternly.

"Now you listen to me," he whispered. "We'll find out what's going on, and you'll be fine. We'll do whatever it takes. I'll give them anything they ask in return for the answers, and you will not try to stop me. Do you hear me? You're going to be fine."

"Ok," I answered weakly.

"Clara," he complained.

"Yes. Ok." I looked up at him and he pulled my forehead to his with a hand on the back of my neck.

"You know what's scaring me most?" he asked. I didn't answer. I knew it was rhetorical. "I ordered you around and you didn't even try to fight back with sarcasm. Where's my snarky Clara at, huh?"

"She's falling asleep," I said and smiled slightly. "I'm sorry."

"Sleep, love. Just sleep." He hugged me tighter. "I'll be right here."

"I know. I love…" I wasn't sure if I finished my thought or not before slipping into sleep.

Nine

The next time I woke, it was daytime again. Enoch and Finn had returned and Eli was fielding questions about what was wrong with me. He just kept telling them to shut up about it.

I lifted my head once they were quiet for a minute. Eli started to smile, but his face went blank. He gripped my face gently and looked at me…before breaking into the biggest grin.

"You're back to normal, baby." He hugged me and released a huge sigh of relief. "You're back to you."

"I am?"

"Yeah." He pulled back and rubbed my cheek with his thumb. "Well, your eyes are. How do *you* feel?"

"Great," I realized. I stretched and smiled. "I feel just fine."

"Well, that's just dandy peaches and rainbow roses, human," Enoch said. "I'm so glad you'll be back to annoying me. Last night was peaceful and quiet with you passed out."

"Shut up, Enoch," Eli told him.

"Yeah, shut up," I repeated.

Eli laughed. "And she's back."

"I guess so," I agreed. "What's next?"

"We should arrive in New Mexico in about an hour. Then we find the Consumed Club, first."

"Why first?"

"Because you can't get into The Wall without a stone from a Witch." I quirked a brow at him to explain. "I'll explain it all later. Put your eyebrow down," he laughed. He seemed more carefree today, compared to the desperation of last night in the bathroom.

"Goblin's teeth, Witch's stones, Consumed Clubs. This trip sounds like a blast already."

"We haven't even gotten to the blood sacrifice part yet," Enoch said and grinned evilly at me.

I balked and looked at Eli, figuring he'd bash Enoch for saying something like that. But he just grimaced shamefully and looked away, his fingers flexing on my hip as a silent apology.

Oh, yeah. A blast...

~ ~ ~

The train jerked to a stop. I felt a fluttering of uneasy butterflies in my gut as Eli took our stuff in one hand and my fingers in the other. We all made our way to the train side and collected our other bag and the bird.

I couldn't be sure, but the bird looked peeved. He watched and eyed us with an intensity that was creepy. First thing Eli said was for us to find a hotel that would accept cash and stash the bird there before making our way to the Consumed Club.

So that's what we did. The clerk at some dive we tried said they had a no-cash policy, but was easily persuaded to accept it - just this once - with a little help from Finn.

"Give me a twenty," Finn told Eli.

Eli grumbled and sighed, then handed over a twenty from his wallet. Finn slipped the twenty into the clerk's hand and he held her fingers a little too long to be considered appropriate. He smiled and asked again, in a - even I had to admit - sexy, alluring voice. "Pretty please, can you take this and let us stay here? We won't be a bother...unless you want *me* to be."

She flushed, her middle aged face perking up at the insinuation. "Just this once."

She took our money and gave him a key. He winked at her as he took it and I thought she'd faint right there. Eli growled under his breath and dragged me to the elevators, bird cage in hand. Finn chuckled and jingled the key and its cracked key ring in his hand as we ascended, the elevator dinging with every passing floor. The fifth was the top and we got off. The smell of *old and gross* hit me and I made a sound in my throat.

"What, princess?" Enoch asked and sneered. "Not up to your high standards?"

"Shut up," Eli said and pushed him. He looked at me when Finn put the key in the lock. "You have to find old places like this where they'll take cash and it won't be so suspicious. Sorry."

"It's ok," I said gently. "I'm fine."

Finn couldn't resist his two cents. "Yes, I find I quite enjoy these old hotels. The smell of sex and sin lingers and stains the air."

Eli sighed harshly before saying, "If you two don't shut the lid on those mouths of yours, we'll hit the trail without you. You wanted to *tag along*," he antagonized Enoch, "so tag along, but seriously, shut up before I shut you up."

"So touchy," Finn said as the door lock clicked loudly. "I don't remember you being so asininely sensitive."

"That was before," Enoch said and laughed. "Before he snagged a conscience that's five foot four, talks too much and reeks of human trouble."

"Five foot five," I rebutted.

"Ok," Eli said in exasperation. "Bloody, ok!" He looked at me with a 'please help, don't hinder' look. "Can we all go in and stop the bickering? I feel like a bloody chaperone."

"You are a bloody chaperone," Enoch countered and glared at me. "When does playtime start?"

"Enough!" He turned me toward the bathroom and pushed me gently. "Go take a long, hot shower. We need to get going at sun down."

"Fine," I muttered. "But I'm only going quietly because I really need a shower."

"That's not going quietly," Enoch mumbled.

"Thank you, CB," Eli said sweetly.

I felt kind of bad for him. I guess he probably did feel like our babysitter. He knew that Finn and Enoch were going to be themselves, and thus annoying, the whole trip and still he let them come because he thought they might help us get the answers we needed. All for me. I sighed and felt guilty, especially after he was so sweet on the train. "Eli, come here."

"Run, boy. The princess is calling," Enoch mocked.

Eli rounded the corner to the bathroom and looked at me expectantly. I leaned in and mouthed a 'sorry' before pulling him down to me and kissing him. It was like someone threw a lit match on me. I had an overwhelming urge to have Eli, make him mine in every way, consume him. It was deep inside me, in my gut and being. It made no sense.

I'd never felt something so strong and almost as if I wasn't even myself anymore before...

Eli recognized my urgency as I clung to him, pulling him through the door and slamming his back to the wall. He groaned as he tried to detach himself from me, but I was having none of that.

I jumped, wrapping my legs around his waist and kissed him opened mouthed and willing for anything. He turned and pressed me to the back of the door and kissed me, but it was reserved. Like he knew something was up, but didn't want to hurt my feelings. But how did I know that?

"Clara," he groaned against my mouth. "Love, you were sick not a few hours ago. Come on, let's take it easy."

"I don't want it easy," I said and stumbled in my motions at the voice that left me. Eli, too, leaned back to assess me. He looked seriously puzzled.

"What was that?" he asked in a whisper.

"I just want you," I answered, but again my voice was sultry and deep. And wrong and completely not mine, but the voice kept speaking anyway.

He cleared his throat. "CB…I, uh…" He looked at me closely. He released my legs, setting my feet to the floor and took my face in his hands. "You don't have to pretend anything with me. You don't have to be some…sexy, over the top girl to make me want you."

I huffed, the sting hitting me right in the chest from his words. "Sexy, over the top girl?"

"You are sexy, I didn't mean that. I meant that you don't have to be something you're not with me. I know exactly who you are and that girl…is who I want. And besides, when we finally do decide to do that, it won't be in some dingy bathroom in a hotel room."

I looked around then, taking in my surroundings. The bathroom was utterly disgusting; the tiles peeling and old, dirty and stained from who knew what. I gulped and shivered in disgust at the bathroom and myself. What was I doing?

"I'm sorry," I whispered and said my next words very, very softly. "Get out, ok?"

"CB," he sighed. "I wasn't trying to jilt you. I just…this isn't exactly a romantic place or situation, and I'm not really sure what's going on with you," he said just as softly. "It's not that I don't want you, I'm just trying to-"

"Just get out, ok," I repeated gently and moved back for him to leave.

He stayed planted there for a few rebellious seconds, his breathing loud and thoughtful before he finally relented with a sigh, closing the door with a soft click. I sighed, too, and grabbed a towel to put down on the floor. My bare feet on the tile was making me nauseas. I hadn't seen any of this before when I'd entered the bathroom. I was in some daze or something and now everything was crystal clear and slamming into me was the knowledge that I was no longer in control of myself.

Something was very wrong with me.

The Wall. We needed to get to The Wall to get answers, and tonight was our ticket to doing that. So I jumped in the shower, closing my mind's eye to the disturbing surroundings and the cheap hotel shampoo, and focusing on the end game.

Once I was done, I realized that I'd forgotten my flat iron. Shoot. So I used the blow dryer in the bathroom and let the natural waves of my hair be. I never wore my hair this way anymore. The curls reminded me too much of my mother's hair and it made me sad.

But now, seeing it like this as I stared at myself in the mirror of a strange bathroom, on a quest to a supernatural place looking for a supernatural cure, made me not just sad, but miss her. I missed her an unhealthy amount all of a sudden and it hit me hard. I leaned on the counter and felt the first tear drip from my nose.

If I could just see her, hear her voice, feel the touch of her sweet, soothing hand on my hair just one more time...

I sucked in a startled breath when someone touched my shoulder.

"It's ok. It's just me," Eli said, but frowned when he worried that I might not want him there either. How did I know that?

I went to him slowly, giving him the option to leave if he wanted, but also so he'd know I wasn't attacking him again. Gah, I couldn't even meet his eyes. How embarrassing to act like that...

He opened his arms gratefully and held me for a long time against his chest. It didn't matter that I wasn't wearing any make-up, it didn't matter that I was only wearing a towel, it didn't matter that I had been crying and knew I had atrocious bags under my red eyes.

It. Just. Didn't. Matter.

He shhed me as he squeezed me. I realized I was crying again, and that made me cry harder. I was pathetic.

"Ah, love, you're breaking my heart," he said sadly.

"I'm sorry. I'm sorry, I'm…something is happening to me," I confessed. "You're right. Something is going on and I want it to stop."

"We will figure this out," he said firmly. "Clara, I won't rest until you're well again. And I don't mean you're not well, I mean…I just mean that-"

"I know what you mean," I said and tried to smile. I may have just looked insane, but he seemed a little relieved. "It's ok. There *is* something wrong with me."

He smoothed my hair. "You miss your mom," he commented calmly. "I'm sorry."

"How do you know that?"

"Because you're in a strange place, mentally and physically, and you weren't just sad in here, I felt your sorrow. I haven't felt that sorrow since I met you at the park, and I knew only one thing could cause that; a daughter really, really needing her mum."

I smiled through my tears. "Mum," I murmured. "My mom would have really liked you."

"I would have liked her." He leaned letting his lips touch my ear. "She made a beautiful, loving, breathtaking daughter."

I sobbed. I sobbed so hard into his shoulder as he let me let loose. He didn't ply me with empty words, he just held me, which I needed more than I ever thought possible. His arms, strong and loving, caressed and pressed me until I calmed. Again, I felt that I could barely look at him. I was a basket case the past couple of days and he probably was more than ready to run for the hills.

"Nope. I'm staying right here."

I balked. "How do you know what I'm thinking this time?"

"Now you're feeling guilt and pain. I can only imagine the wild things that female brain is conjuring." He smiled. "I..." He gulped. "I, uh..."

There it was again. That thing that we both wanted so desperately to say to each other and it was right there...but so far away.

"Thank you," I said softly. "I'll get ready so we can go."

"Wear something pretty and...sexy," he said and wrinkled his nose. "We're going to have to put on a production tonight."

"I didn't bring anything pretty or sexy."

"Sure you did," Finn said cockily and grinned from the door. "Good old Finn's here to save the day."

Ten

"Give me your skirt," he ordered.

I handed him my school uniform skirt from the bathroom sink, confused. He took it and rifled through the hotel drawers until he found a pair of scissors. Oh, no.

"You can't cut my skirt! That's my uniform," I argued.

He poised the fabric on the edge of the scissors and paused. "Do you have another?"

"Yes, but-"

He snipped. I bolted into the room and groaned as he finished, taking the hem shorter all the way across, but leaving one side slightly higher than the other on the thighs. Eli stood in front of me to block my toweled body from their eyes. Finn held it up, letting the excess fabric fall away. I wanted to be mad, but…it was so darn cute with the off kilter cut and ruffles, though it was pretty short.

"Why did you do that?" I asked anyway.

"Because you can't go in there all *school girl,* though it is pretty hot. You need to look like a mate does. And a mate looks like someone who wants to please their Devourer. If Eli was your mate, he'd want to dress a certain way."

"I still don't understand."

"Sluts," Enoch provided. "The mates dress like sluts."

"Well put, Mister Tact. Thank you," Finn laughed. "Yes. Sluts."

"Why do they dress that way? Why would my Devourer want me to show all of my goodies to everyone else?"

The bird squawked from the corner, "Goodies. Show 'em your goodies."

They all burst out laughing. Eli tried to stop it with a fist to his mouth, but it was no use. I looked at him and chuckled a little, too. They got the gist though, right?

Finn answered through a laugh, "To show off your mate's *goodies* is to brag to others about what they can't have."

"That's kinda dumb. And not very logical."

"Either way, go put this on."

He held it out to me. Eli took the skirt and held it up before looking back at me with a frown. "You don't have to wear this."

"I want to blend in as much as possible…wait! What about the string? How are we going to hide it there?"

"Well," Eli drawled and turned to me. "For one, I'm not letting you out of my sight and you're not leaving my side. For two, we'll both wear long sleeves and hold hands. It's so dark and smoky, no one will notice."

"Are you sure? But what about Enoch's string?"

He groaned and bit his lip as he thought. "It won't be something they'll be looking for. We should still be fine."

"Ok," I agreed. "I'll get changed."

"So will we," Finn said as he began to unbutton his shirt. "You aren't the only one who needs to look good. Eli, I'm snagging a shirt."

I grabbed my bag and closed the bathroom door without saying anything. I put on my make-up and clothes. There was only a sink mirror, not a full length, so I had no idea what I looked like head to toe, but above the shoulders was acceptable. After slipping in my silver wing earrings, I put back on Ariel's boots. I could only assume it worked for the look I was going for.

My skirt was short, but it seemed to look cute as I looked down at myself. I picked a red long sleeve, tight sweater that I usually wore under my uniform vest. It worked, so I opened the door, but Eli and Enoch were gone.

"Where's Eli?" I asked.

Finn jerked his gaze to me in an uninterested motion, but then did a not-so-subtle double take. He straightened from where he was doing the laces on his boots.

"Can I just say…Wow."

"Stop," I complained and tried to pull my skirt down further. "Where's Eli?"

"He went to get you a soda," he advised, never removing his eyes from me.

"Where's Enoch?"

"Enoch is Enoch. He goes where he wants to."

He moved towards me, every inch the predator he was. I tried not to gulp as he stalked me across the room. My back hit the wall and I waited with my hands out as he slammed into me with his chest, his hands moving mine to my sides with inhuman speed. His face was not even an inch from mine as he watched me with blazing purple eyes. He licked his bottom lip and I couldn't remember ever being so scared in my life as he made a low noise in his throat.

He didn't care about me at all. He thought I ruined Eli, tricked him somehow. And now, Eli was nowhere to be seen and Finn apparently had something up his sleeve.

"Eli told me to test you," he told me.

"Test me? Test me how?"

Enoch came through the door with a loud bang. We both jerked our attention to him and he stopped. He smiled and chuckled under his breath. "So, he really asked you to do it?" he asked Finn.

"Yes. Now please leave so I can get on with it."

He left and I felt my heart jump at the implication. "Get on with what?" I asked breathlessly.

And then he pushed his lips to mine.

I was overwhelmed with a sense of need to kiss him. It was like it was planted there, but I could sense it and recognize it for what it was. Finn was forcing lust on me, or out of me, whatever, but it wasn't working the way he planned. I felt it, harnessed it, and pushed it back to him.

Well, that was a huge mistake.

He was definitely fueled by my actions and instead of trying to feed himself off of my fear and need, he was...feeding me his. I felt it as he pulled me to him and used his lips in caresses instead of harsh, biting moves. He groaned and let one of his hands move from my hand to the back of my neck.

I wasn't kissing him back, but he didn't seem to notice or care. I tried to push him off when I realized what he was doing, but I was too late and too weak. He opened my mouth, tilting my head to the side and letting himself in. I pushed harder against his chest and heard my noise of complaint, but he kept at it.

The idea seemed to plant itself in my mind, like it was its own entity, its own force: Make him fear me. So I thought of the scariest thing I could think of at the moment. I remembered what it felt like to think that car was going to hit me. I remembered the fear and anguish on the woman's face - even though it had all be fabricated by Finn - it was real enough to me. I let it loose on him, and when he whimpered, I knew I had him.

He jerked back and looked at me with wide, fearful eyes. He went backwards until he sank onto the bed. "How the hell did you do that?" he said, his voice hateful and loathsome as he looked at me.

"Do what?" I said innocently.

"You know what? How did you do that? Answer me!" he yelled and began to come at me again, with a whole new set of intentions.

Of course, that would be the moment my Eli came back.

I heard the growl from the door and watched as Eli slammed Finn into the back wall. His body left an imprint in the plaster and a tacky picture next to them fell, shattering the glass to the floor.

Finn wasn't even fighting back as he watched me from over Eli's shoulder. "What are you doing, Finn?"

"Not a thing," Finn drawled, shoving Eli away from him. "I'll meet you at the club."

He left, keeping his eyes on me at all times. He slammed the door and I jumped as I fought to steady my breath after what just happened. Eli came to me quickly and pulled me to him with a sigh of relief. "Baby, I'm so sorry." He leaned back and looked horribly guilty. Too bad it didn't help anything. "Love, say something. Did he hurt you? What happened?"

"Where's my soda?" I sneered, my hands shaking with anger as I pushed his hands off of me.

"Oh," he said and looked around in confusion, "I must have dropped it in the hall when I saw Finn coming for you. I had to walk all the way over to the… What's the matter?" He sucked in a breath and gritted his teeth. "You're pretty livid. Please calm down."

"Why? I can still feed you this way, can't I?" I asked and gritted my teeth, too. "Anger is still a food group for you."

He made a noise between pleasure and pain and then commanded in a stern voice, "Stop, Clara. I don't want to feed off of your anger. What's the matter with you? You're acting like you're angry with me instead of Finn."

"Should I be?"

"Why would you be?" he asked incredulously, his pierced brow jumping.

"Whatever." I took a deep breath. "Let's go."

"Not until you tell me what's wrong."

I pushed his chest once more, harder this time to get him to move. "I want to go. Now."

He looked torn. Was he really going to pretend that he hadn't asked Finn to test me? Kiss me? Even Enoch knew about it. It boiled my blood all over again and I stalked towards the door. "I'll be waiting outside."

"Fine," he fired back and held his hands up in surrender as he went to his bag.

I made my way down the hall and waited near the front door for him. Enoch was nowhere to be seen, Finn was gone, thank heavens. The clerk eyed me - well, he eyed my skirt - with intrigue. I glared back at him. He was new. Their shifts must have changed. He smiled at my glare, seeming to be amused by it.

Eli bolted from the stairs and searched the room quickly for me. Once his eyes found me he tried to act like he hadn't just been searching frantically for me. It almost warmed my heart. Almost. I couldn't remember being so pissed before. My insides were fighting for the forefront. I wanted to just forgive him. He probably had a reason, he always did, but there was another part of me that wanted to just be angry.

"Ready?" he asked.

"Yep."

"We've got to take a taxi."

"I figured."

He sighed and led the way. He held the door open for me and then a taxi pulled into the driveway. I looked at him in question. This wasn't exactly New York where taxies jumped on the curb to give you a ride.

"I called them while I was getting you a drink," he advised as he swung his arm for me to enter the cab first.

I hopped in, attempting to keep my skirt covering everything as I did so. Eli explained to the cabbie where we wanted to go before turning to me. He reached out and took my fingers in his hand slowly. "I didn't get a chance to tell you how great you look."

"You were busy, I guess, making sure everything was thoroughly handled, right?"

His eyes went wide. "I just gave you a compliment, love. How can you possibly be mad at me?"

I huffed and turned to stare out the window. I felt him caressing my promise ring with his thumb. It burned at his touch. I jerked my hand back in aggravation.

Then the next words out of his mouth were the dumbest words any human male could utter, but then, he wasn't human, was he? "Did we forget to bring some medication for you? Is it that time of the month? Because I am completely confused right now."

I felt my face flush with heat. I wasn't embarrassed, I was just about to go ape-crap on him. I looked at him slowly, but before I could say anything, the cabbie beat me to it.

"Ah, man, you're such an idiot," he said and chuckled in that you're-so-gonna-get-it way.

I decided to not say anything and watched as the scenery flew by out my window. If I spoke, I wasn't sure what would come out of my mouth. Eli stayed silent, too, on his side of the car. When we arrived at the club, I wasn't impressed, but I could feel a weird hum around me. I knew it was the place.

We were at the Consumed Club, Eli had asked his 'friend'- who he knew hated me- to kiss me for a test of some sort, his brother hated me, too, and was here as well. Eli rejected my advances, my skirt was ruined, I was dressed like a hooker, Eli was on my crap list, and the only one who seemed to be on my side was the freaking cabbie.

Eleven

The air was teeming with energy, smoke and all sorts of creatures I never knew existed.

Eli had pulled me from the cab and said he didn't understand what I was so upset about, but he needed to lay down some ground rules. I wasn't supposed to have 'the sight', which was being able to see how things really were instead of what was being glamoured for me to see. He said just to try not to stare at anybody or anything and, even though I was mad, I had to stick to his side.

He said we couldn't stay too long because the Elves smoked and the smoke was intoxicating, especially to humans. It made you be crazy, he said. I was barely listening to him. I was just ready to go in.

There was no doorman and the building looked heinous from the outside. No one would ever think to go there for a party, but once Eli opened the back door in the alley, the low light and smoke hit us. I sucked in a startled breath at the burn in my lungs. And the music pounded when moments ago, I could hear not a sound outside. It didn't make sense, but I guess that was the point.

Eli held my hand as we entered the room. Our long sleeves covered our wrists and he was right. The lights were so low, you could barely see anything. But what I could see scared the hebedejebedees out of me. There were Witches, Elves, and all sorts of other creatures. And the only way I knew what they were is because it looked like Halloween was in full swing.

The Witches were short, stocky and ugly. Their noses were long and over pronounced, just like cartoons made them out to be. The Elves were tall and too slim, their ears pointy and large. They smiled, showing teeth that were big and white as they guffawed over a card game. The others, I wasn't sure what they were, but you could tell something was off.

And then the humans were easy to spot.

The girls were skinny and pretty, or you could tell that they used to be. And Enoch and Finn had been correct in that they were all dressed in barely-there clothing. The human men were the same, wearing no shirts or just tanks and jeans. They clung to their Devourers like lovesick animals who couldn't be separated, hanging on their every word, even when they weren't speaking to them.

I cringed and knew that I was supposed to be acting that way or people, and I used that term really loosely, would be suspicious soon. Eli stopped at the bar and ordered us waters. I draped my arm around his neck and let our chests touch. Eli looked at me with a dull expression as his hands went to my hips loosely. So he understood what I was doing. He knew I wasn't over my fit yet, and he apparently was a little peeved himself.

Good.

The bartender gave us our waters and when he spoke, he hissed like a snake with his words. "Six dollars, Devourer."

And then a long, snake like tongue emerged from his mouth. I gripped Eli tighter as he paid, not turning away from me. I tried not to look at the snake man. I didn't know if I was supposed to be able to see that or not. Eli, ever the gentleman even if he was mad, opened my water bottle for me and rubbed a soothing hand down my arm to tell me it was all right.

I took a big sip, letting the cool take some of the edge of the heat off. The room was stifling and crowded. I closed my eyes and enjoyed a moment's peace, but Eli stopped me. "Don't do that."

"What?"

"Don't give them the opportunity to drag you into a reverie. Some Devourers who like to cause trouble would do it just to start a fight with me."

He nodded to a group of Devourers in the corner. They watched the room, circling it with their eyes.

"Oh." I cleared my throat. "Ok. Now what?"

"Now we find a Witch who'll give us a stone."

"What do we have to do for it?"

"That's what we need to find out." He slipped an arm around my waist and pressed his face into my neck. "I'm going to have to treat you like I would my mate. They don't always play nice, but it's just an act. I want to make that perfectly clear. I'm not doing this because we're in a spat. I need them all to believe and if they don't, even for a second, we're in trouble. So you can't be obstinate to me, not even a little. You have to act as though you want me like nothing else, even if that's not actually true right now. Do you understand?"

I leaned back and smiled coyly. I rose up to kiss his neck and let him know without words that I heard him loud and clear. He tried not to respond, but he didn't last long. He sighed raggedly, pulling me closer, and murmuring something I couldn't hear over the depressing music. I leaned back to see him and saw how torn he was about everything. I was bumped by someone who came to the bar. She grinned at the bartender and asked for something in a different language. She leaned over the bar to flirt with him and I saw it. She had a tail.

Eli turned us away from the bar and I tried to remind myself not to notice these things. We spotted Enoch and Finn in the back chatting up some others there. They were laughing and carrying on about something. Finn had a girl in his lap, but she was not human. Her ears and chin were too pointy, and her skin was too white. She laughed, throwing her head back and wiggling solicitously on his lap. It was then I saw her fangs. I turned to Eli's chest and stared at it.

This was impossible. How was I supposed to pretend not to see any of this? "Let's find a Witch and get out of here."

"Doesn't work like that," he said dully. Then he looked at me and noticed my paleness, my general fright and want to be anywhere but there. His face visibly softened. "We have to play the part, Clara. No one comes to a Consumed Club for five minutes. And whatever the Witch wants as payment will probably be an act, not a possession."

"Like what?"

He shook his head. "We'll see. In the mean time," he let his sentence drift off as he inched closer. I knew I couldn't stop him from kissing me and so did he. I narrowed my eyes a little to let him know that I knew what he was doing. He kept coming and touched my lips so gently with his. His hands gripped me tightly and passionately, but his lips were feather light and sweet. He was putting on a show.

I kissed him back. Mad or not, those lips would not be denied. I let my arm - the unbonded one - encircle his neck and he lifted me against him for a moment before putting my feet back to the ground and releasing me. He stopped kissing me so quickly I almost stumbled. I looked up to him to see him looking bored around the room. Oh, right. He was supposed to treat me like he wanted me one second and like crap the next. Check.

I draped myself on his arm and tried to mimic what I saw from the other mates. It was infuriating and pathetic. They looked sick and drugged…and then I saw them doing drugs. Or at least I thought they were drugs. One Devourer held a baggie with one little purple pill inside it over her head and made her beg for it, like a dog. Then he opened it and placed it on her tongue. She swallowed it easily and kissed his feet before standing and dancing around him. He watched joyfully, a sniveling smile on his lips. She made her way back to his front and trailed her hand down his chest. He snatched her to him and kissed her roughly, but she sighed, sinking into him with needy desperation. They danced together and others joined in.

The music was something I'd never heard before, but it's what I imagined Devourers would listen to. It was grungy, screaming voices, banging drums and guitars with no rhyme or reason. And the dancing was dirty.

I'd seen Dirty Dancing and crushed on Patrick Swayze like every other girl in America, but this was so much dirtier than that. I had to look away to keep myself from blushing. But then Eli began to move against me and I realized we had been standing in the middle of the dance floor the whole time.

I didn't want to dance, but didn't see a way out of it. So I let Eli sling my arm around his neck and kept the other one attached to his. He tilted my head back, kissing my throat and then biting my skin in playful teasing for all to see.

A girl with green hair and cat eyes was suddenly pressing herself to Eli's back. Her arms snaked around his back to his front and she licked his ear. I waited for him to push her off, but he actually grinned at her over his shoulder. I felt a stab of not just anger, but red hot, boiling jealousy blare through me.

Then I felt an extra set of hands on my hips and a face nuzzling my hair from behind. I tried to turn to see who or what it was, but it was too crowded and he was behind me. But he was dancing in rhythm to me and if Eli wanted to play along, then fine. I started moving with him and felt a smidge of triumph when Eli glared at the man over my shoulder. What was good for the gander was good for the goose, wasn't it?

Apparently not.

"Beat it," Eli growled.

I turned as he turned away without another word and saw that he was a half man-half beast…thing. He had animal legs. I quickly set my gaze back on Eli, who was now alone with me and the gyrating bodies around us. Green hair was gone and it was a good thing; I was in no mood to be polite anymore.

"What? Upset that my hands are the only ones left now?" he asked hotly.

"No. Are you upset that I'm the only one pressed against you?"

"No," he growled and leaned close so no one could hear us. "I thought I explained all of this-"

"You didn't explain that you were going to let other girls lick you," I shot back in a hiss.

"We do things like that, Clara. We all dance together."

"That's what I was doing, too, but you sent him away."

"Mates don't flirt with anyone else."

I huffed. "But it's ok for Devourers?"

He shrugged. "Yes. It is. I told you that this wasn't going to be fun. I told you that this was a mission for us, not a party."

"You didn't tell me that you were going to have Finn kiss me, testing me, and then parade me through all of these supernatural things while you let other girls kiss you!" My breaths rushed in and out loudly as I waited for him to start explaining it away again, but instead he stood stunned.

And then he dragged me across the room, through the crowd and all the way to the back bathrooms. They were both busy, so he shoved me into a cleaning closet. The murderous look on Eli's face was enough of an indicator that he wasn't to be toyed with right now.

"Now," he growled and slammed the door, throwing the bolt into place, "you explain what you said to me out there."

"This is ridiculous," I said back and paced around the small room. "Don't even pretend that you didn't let that girl-"

"Pixie!" he yelled. "She was a Pixie!"

"Pixie. Whatever. Don't pretend that you didn't let her kiss you! And then you smiled at her!"

"I was playing a part, I've explained that. What I want is for you to tell me," he came forward and stopped me with his hands on my arms, "in great detail what you meant by saying that I had Finn kiss you." His jaw was taut and angry.

"Finn said-"

"There's mistake number one: Finn said."

"And Enoch said!" I countered. "They both said that you told Finn to kiss me, to test me."

"Test you for what?" he asked in exasperation. "Answer me," he said angrily as I stayed quiet.

"I don't know!"

"Clara," he said and took a deep breath. "Clara, I want to punch something for just listening to you say the words. I would never, ever, ever, tell someone else, especially a Devourer, to put his lips on you." He paused and shook his head. "Please tell me he didn't put his lips on you."

"He kissed me," I said, not sure what to believe anymore. "You didn't tell him to test me? You promise?"

"Clara, would you describe me as possessive?"

"Yes-"

"Then how could you have ever thought that I'd tell someone else to kiss you, to take what is mine."

"I..." Wow. I felt the last couple hours of strain and doubt crumble around me. I wasn't thinking clearly. I was being stupid. I was letting others make my decisions for me once again. "I'm..."

"He kissed you on the mouth?"

"Yes," I whispered.

"I'll be right back," he said low and dangerously.

"Don't," I said in rush and grabbed his arm. "You can't go out there without me and I don't want you to start a fight here. We need to get the Witch's stone."

"He can't get away with this. He was trying to test you, to see if you'd fall for his sway and then try to get me angry about the fact that you kissed him back. He used his lust on you?"

"Yeah. I could feel it."

He groaned unhappily. "Then you did kiss him back." He shook his head. "It wasn't your fault. You can't control yourself when we-"

"No, I didn't kiss him back. Something…happened." He looked puzzled. "I could feel the way he pushed the emotion on me, trying to make me feel it. But I pushed it back." His brow pulled down in a frown. "I made him feel it instead and he…" I bit my lip.

"He what?" he whispered.

"He lost it. He kissed me for real and I scared him to get him to stop. That's why he was coming after me when you came in. He was angry because of what I'd done. Eli, something's wrong with me. I can feel something…pulling in me."

"How could you have done that?" he asked and looked closely in my eyes. "Still green," he murmured to himself.

"I don't know. But I didn't kiss him."

"I need to…" He groaned again.

"What?"

"I need to see Finn."

"It won't do any good," I argued.

"It will."

"How?"

"Because I need to hit something."

I stared up at him and it was the first time all day that I felt like laughing. So I did. I really wanted to let him loose on Finn and punch his jaw for what he did to me. Especially since him and Enoch lied to me! They flat lied to make me think Eli had done that. I was furious, but it was also funny with ridiculousness.

He cracked a small smile, too, and chuckled under his breath. I wrapped my arms around his neck in apology. "I'm sorry," I said simply, but sincerely.

"Love, look at me." I did. "I'm not scolding you, but how could you think that I'd-"

"You're right." I nodded. "You're right. Something is very wrong with me. I mean how could I make him feel-"

"No more right now." He closed his eyes tightly. "I'm going to figure all of this out tonight, if we don't do anything else." He framed my face with his warm hands. "Please believe that. I don't want to think about what's going on with you because I'll break apart, but if we keep moving forward and get the stone so we can get into The Wall, we can get answers. I know it. Please just trust me. I didn't want that Pixie's hands on me, you have to know that. And I'm probably not going to want to do what the Witch wants either, but I'll do it. I'll do anything for you." I felt my lip quiver with gratitude. He grinned sadly. "But let a Satyr puts his paws on you? That I won't do."

I laughed and hurried to wipe my eyes before my tears messed up my make-up. Mates didn't cry in broom closets, I was sure. Major mate faux pas. He tore a piece of tissue and gently wiped under my eyes for me. He was always taking care of me in ways like that.

"Thank you," I said and grabbed his hands to make him look at me. "Thank you," I said slower for emphasis. I reached up on my tip toes to kiss him. "I'm really sorry," I said against his lips.

"It's forgotten, love," he replied and encircled me with his arms. "I'm sorry, too."

He lifted me and set me on the counter as he continued to kiss me. He held my face gently and stood between my knees, his mouth devouring me in more ways than one. I pulled him closer with my fist in his shirt and he complied happily.

He pulled back a little and licked his lip before looking down at me. "Is it all right to tell you how hot you look now?"

"Yes," I giggled.

Someone banged on the door, but we ignored them as he kissed me again. They kept banging. When they yelled a 'Hey' and began to wrench on the doorknob, Eli was done.

He kicked the door with his boot. "It's taken! Take a hint, buddy!"

We both laughed as we heard him grumbling on the other side of the door.

"We better get out of here," he continued. "Let's steer clear of Finn until we get what we need, because I will be having words with him. And fists, too. Don't try to stop it."

"Be my guest."

"All right. Let's go find us a Witch." He helped me down from the counter top and unlatched the door, but stopped. "You're doing good pretending that they don't freak you out."

"Which ones am I not supposed to see?"

"Well, most of them don't care in the club, but it's not really the people you don't see, it's just that you don't really care, I guess. It should be second nature to see those things and not care because you're so consumed with me, your Devourer," he explained carefully.

"Well," I smiled, "now that I'm not mad at you, I shouldn't have a problem with that."

"Ha ha." He grinned, but it slowly faded away as he got serious. "Now things will probably start to get fuzzy to you. The Elves are smoking double time tonight and their smoke removes your inhibitions and control. We need to stay focused and get what we need quickly. Witches are not to be toyed with. They are evil and manipulative; every bad thing you can think of. They'll probably try to offer you all kinds of things, so just let me talk or be coy if someone talks directly to you. Just be flighty."

"Flighty. Got it," I sighed. I squeezed my eyes shut as a new headache started to build. Oh, no. The worst possible time.

"Hey. Love?" He lifted my chin. "You all right?"

"I will be," I said firmly. "Let's just go do this. I'll be ok."

He kissed me once more and rested his forehead to mine. "You'll be ok," he repeated. "You can't leave me. You'll be ok."

I didn't refute him or agree. I just accepted his comfort and let him lead me from the room. A group of annoyed creatures who were waiting for the bathroom awaited us in the hall when he opened the door. Eli smiled smugly at them and took my hand as he led me down the hall.

I wanted to roll my eyes at them, knowing exactly what they were thinking. When we reached the dance floor again, he put his front to my back this time as he moved us to sway our way through the packed crowd.

We were stuck in the packed bodies and the heat was almost unbearable. I felt sweat dripping down my back under my long sleeve shirt. Eli pulled my hair away from my neck and blew his breath to cool me as we swayed. Goose bumps made their way down my arms and legs and I giggled. He leaned forward, letting his lips touch my neck. I felt his tongue and leaned back against him.

"Your sweat is sweet," he murmured and kissed me again. I opened my eyes and saw another Pixie girl in front of me. She reached over me to Eli, as if I wasn't even there between them. He pushed her hand away carelessly and said, "Not this time. My hands are full."

Then he turned me to him and unleashed the full force of his mouth on mine. It was like being drunk - well, what I assumed being drunk would feel like. I was hot, but I shivered and felt light as air, but also like I could barely hold myself up. He took care of that as he held me in his arms, crossing them on my back and backside as if to shield me from other hands and eyes.

We finally made a little progress in the crowd and Eli released me. He gave me a long assessing look to check on me. I nodded slightly, licking my lips and tasting the salt of our skin there.

We went to the bar again and ordered something called a 'Worry Wart'. When he took it from the bar, it steamed and the smell almost made me gag. Eli looked at me sympathetically before carefully taking the drink to a nearby table.

I straightened my back and wiped my face clear of any expression except loving adoration for my Devourer as he set the drink on the table in front of a Witch.

Showtime.

Twelve

"A Witch's brew?" she said and I struggled not to wince at her words. Her voice was grating, scratchy and high to the point of being painful to my eardrums. "You have a request for me, Devourer?"

"I do," he said calmly. "I want a stone."

"Of course you do," she said sarcastically and cackled as the Elves laughed around her. She was short, dark skinned and round where the Elves were tall, seriously pale and too skinny. It was a drastic contrast. She downed the drink in one gulp, but the glass sizzled and crackled as if it'd shatter when she put it back to the table empty. "They always want a stone."

"Just tell me what I have to do," Eli answered back, unfazed.

"I'm not sure if I'm in a stone giving mood, Devourer. I've already got my drink. What else would I need from you?"

"The drink was to butter you up, Witch." He gripped my hand tightly, soothingly. "Give me the task and I'll do it."

"Oooh," she crooned and leaned back in her seat leisurely. Her nose was too big for her face, her eyes small and black, her skin dry with wrinkles and blemishes. And she was wearing a moo-moo of some sort. A freaking moo-moo! "I like the sound of that. What do you say gents?" She looked at the three Elves sitting at her table. I suppressed a cough as they blew smoke our way. "Should we bargain for a little entertainment?"

Eli stiffened next to me. "Entertainment isn't what I had in mind for payment."

"Beggars can't be choosers, now can they, Devourer?"

Eli rumbled low in his chest. "No, I guess not."

"Let's see," she thought, letting her long, dirty nails scratch at the wood of the table. "Show your mate to me."

"No," Eli said clearly, pulling me behind him just a bit. "She has nothing to do with this and I'm not into sharing."

She laughed and shook her head in chastisement of him. "Aye, we've touched a nerve. You Devourers; so stingy and superior. If you'd open your minds up to the possibilities-"

"Not. Going. To. Happen."

She held up her hands. "Ok. Show her to us anyway."

He paused for a few seconds before pulling my hand and moving me in front of him. He grimaced as he lifted a finger and turned it in a circle in the air, indicating for me to turn for them. I looked up at him and did as he asked, only looking away when I wasn't facing him, but latching back onto his gaze once I was. He never removed his eyes as he said to them, "That's all you're going to get."

I felt hands on my shoulders and then I was turned. She was in my space, her rancid breath on my face. She looked up into my face because I was taller than her. "You have some amazing green eyes."

"My Eli thinks so," I answered coolly.

She smirked…I think. "I bet he does. How long has she been with you?" she asked Eli.

"Not long," he answered.

"She's in deep, Elijah." She looked at him over my shoulder. "My, my how you've reined her in quickly."

He growled, pulling me behind him again. "And when was it that you figured out who I was?"

"The second your twin came in before you and wasn't shy on the family details." She cackled again and everyone else followed suit. We had a small crowd gathered around us now, and they watched us eagerly.

""The richest, meanest, self-proclaimed kingship Devourer family walks in and you think we wouldn't take notice?"

"I am not part of the family anymore. Isn't that what the clubs are for? Rogues?" Eli said hotly.

"Or recruits for the Horde?" someone yelled out.

"Yes. That, too," the Witch agreed. "Are you a Horde spy?"

"Why would I spy for them? I hate them. Who's leading the Horde these days? Hatch is toast."

"His second in command," she informed before sucking snot loudly into her throat and spitting it on the floor. "Reece. He's been here. He was here two days ago looking for something."

"What? Why would the Horde care what goes on in a Consumed Club?"

"The Horde is getting more and more hoity. They think they act for rebels, but have become the very thing they despise by working so diligently to rule everyone."

"You're preaching to the choir, Witch," Eli explained.

"Good," she said and everyone seemed to calm. It seemed as though they'd been waiting on a fight, but that one word diffused it. "Now. Payment. Hmmm..."

"I can offer you cash."

"This isn't a negotiation," she barked and Eli sighed as he stood quietly. Waiting. "How about she demonstrates what happens when a human consumes the smoke outright? We haven't seen anyone that crazy in a long while!" She laughed.

"Nope," Eli muttered.

"Come on, feeler," she teased me and held a brown rolled smoke out. "Take a puff. You won't remember a thing."

"If she survives," Eli growled. "I told you, she has nothing to do with it." He pulled me to his side and I looked up at him in surprise. He smirked at me and then looked blandly at them. "I like her to be clear headed. I want her to feel and remember everything when she's with me. No drugs for her."

"Boo," she complained and pouted. "You're taking all of our fun."

"I'll do anything you want, however," he said.

"Hmm," she thought. "I think a stone is worth more than that. I think a sacrifice is needed here."

Eli remained calm, though his fingers squeezed mine. I wondered if he was seeking comfort as much as he was trying to give it. "What's the offering?"

"Skin," she said and grinned.

"Skin?" he breathed and huffed.

"Yep. Skin."

He stuck is arm out and said through gritted teeth. "Let's get on with it then."

"No, no, no. Not yours." Eli shook his head before she even said the words, but it was pretty obvious what she was hinting at. And when she finally said it, Eli sagged. "Hers."

"No," he barked. "I said no." He paused, thinking. "I don't want her marred and scarred. I want her skin perfect, just like it is."

"And I want her skin under my knife," the Witch said casually. I felt my jaw drop when it finally seemed to sink in. Knife? She was going to cut off my skin?

"No," he growled.

"Then no stone."

Eli turned to leave, but I didn't let him pull me. I needed this. *We* needed this. If we didn't get to The Wall, then I'd never know what was wrong with me and I had no interest in staying bi-polar with headaches that crippled me. "Wait. I'll do it."

"No, you will not. Get your butt out that door," he told me harshly and argued with his eyes as I looked at him.

"Let me do it," I mouthed to him. "Please."

"No," he mouthed back to me.

"Elijah Thames, you let her offer her own sacrifice!" she said harshly. "That's not your place."

"She's mine," he rebutted just as harshly. "You can't tell me what to do with what's mine!"

"Let the girl decide," one of the Elves said as he puffed smoke into the air in rings. His long legs were perched on the table. "She seems perfectly competent."

"What do I have to do?" I interrupted.

The Witch stood and took my arm in her hands. Eli gripped my other arm tighter. I bit my lip as I realized that he may not have wanted to do this because it made it more liable for them to see the string. "Beautiful, supple skin," she murmured.

One of the Elves in the back stood and reached down into his boot, unsheathing a small silver knife. He handed it to the Witch and she gripped it delicately in her fingers. "You're offering a sacrifice of skin to me freely?"

"Yes," I answered, but quickly added, "in exchange for a stone."

She grinned. "That's a good girl."

"No," Eli said from behind me and tried to pull me back. "No!" he repeated, but it was futile. My feet were glued to the floor by some force the Witch was using. "It's the smoke, Clara. You don't really want to do it."

"I want to help," I muttered and watched in strange fascination as she waved the blade over the skin of the underside of my forearm.

She let the blade touch my skin and I jolted as the blade was freezing cold. She smiled evilly and let it touch my skin again. Then she dragged the blade in a downward motion, like taking the skin off of fruit. It hurt when she broke the skin and went deeper, but I couldn't scream. I heard Eli struggling, but he couldn't pull me. My body just watched in horror. When she was done, she picked up the layer of skin she'd cut and eyed it like a prize. She set it on the table and looked back at me, but stopped. Her face changed. I looked down to see what she saw and gasped.

My red blood was flowing down my arm in a stream from both sides...but there was also a stream of blue. It didn't mix or mingle with my blood, they just existed separately.

Then Eli was released and he bumped into my back as if he'd been let go by someone. Enoch was there, too, and none too happy. The bond must have pulled him to me. Eli pulled me to him, but not before seeing my arm. The Witch eyed us both with accusing eyes. "What's this?"

"It looks like..." Enoch said.

"Devourer blood," she whispered. "I know. How does the feeler girl have it? It's impossible."

"I don't...know," Eli said and looked at the blood in horror. "I don't know."

"I like you, Elijah Thames." She picked up my skin and laid the slice of skin on her own forearm. "And I like you, too, feeler. You've got spunk." The skin began to merge and attach itself to hers. She smiled and closed her eyes. The skin layer grew and covered her whole arm, and then went up to cover her neck and face. She had new skin. My skin...She transformed into this young...pretty girl that you could tell something was off, but just couldn't put your finger on it. "So, I'm going to give you a head start from the Horde," she muttered as she opened her eyes. "I never liked the way the Witches' council tried to rule us either and am glad they were eradicated so long ago." She shook her head. "I don't know how you altered her the way you have, but you won't make it long. Meet my fetcher boy at the corner of Liam and Pike tomorrow at dawn. Go," she warned.

Eli wasted no time. He dragged me closely behind him. I heard a few curses as he plowed through the people. He never once looked back for Finn, but Enoch was right on our tail. We slammed out of the doors and I thought we'd call another cab, but Eli stopped and pulled me to his chest. "Hang on tight."

I did and then we were going inhumanly fast. He blurred us with Enoch following all the way back to the hotel parking lot. We stopped in the side alley next to the trash bins. The first breath I took was filled with garbage smell and I thought I'd vomit. I clung to Eli as I fought to get my bearings.

Then I remembered what had happened. I had Devourer blood in me. How? What did it mean?

I looked up at Eli and he was looking at me with a deep frown. Enoch was already gone. I let my gaze fall to the cracked pavement below us and felt shameful for no good reason at all.

Eli lifted my arm and sighed. "We need to get this taken care of."

"Ok," I said softly and turned to go.

He sucked in a swift breath and grabbed my hand. "Wait, sweetheart." I turned to him and peeked from under my lashes. "I'm sorry," he said and I straightened. He hugged me to him. "I'm so sorry. I couldn't do anything. I tried to stop her."

"I let her to do it. We needed her to."

"You let her because of the Elf smoke. It makes you feel like you can do anything and it won't matter." He shook his head. "I'm sorry."

"I'm ok," I said and turned to go again.

"Wait. Where are you going?" he said in exasperation.

"To the room." I rubbed my temples. "I just want to sleep."

"We need to talk about this, Clara. We can't pretend that didn't just happen."

"I have Devourer blood," I said like a confession. "I don't know what that means, or what's happening, but it's my fault."

"How is it your fault?" he asked and pulled me to him once more. "Clara, come on."

"Because I was trying to be sexy or sultry or...something." I sniffed and looked up to him to see if he was making the same conclusion as I was. "That day the Horde came and you pricked your finger. I...put it in my mouth to make it feel better. Remember?"

"I'll never forget that, even if I live to be five thousand."

"That was it. I did this. I made myself sick somehow by mixing our bloods and it's all my fault."

"So, because you tried to make me feel better, you deserve to be sick. That's what you're saying?" he asked and shook his head, looking at me with love shining through his eyes.

I felt the tears come and couldn't even be embarrassed by them. It was like whatever my body felt, it just went for it and didn't worry about consequences.

He lifted me in his arms and carried me to our room. I pressed my face into his neck and cried out everything that I felt. Enoch was watching UFC on the TV when we entered. I saw him roll his eyes when we passed by. Eli took me to the bathroom and set me on the toilet lid. "Stay," he commanded softly.

I sat there and saw him rummage through my bag before coming back. He took a bottle out as he squatted in front of me and looked at it. Then he tore open a small package, spilled the peroxide on it and swiped the cotton ball across my skin. It stung, but I didn't flinch. He pressed the cloth bandage to my arm and then stood again, going into the room.

I felt my mouth fall open when I realized what he was doing. He grabbed a pillow and the snatched the comforter off the bed. He brought it back to the bathroom and laid it all out in the large tub like a bed or pallet. He shut and locked the door before kicking off his boots and then kneeling at my feet.

He lifted one foot and removed my boot gently. He watched me watch him as he removed the next one and then kissed the sole of my stocking covered foot. I felt like I should blush, but it never came. He got on both knees between mine and looked at me seriously.

"Will you sleep with me?" he asked softly, before grinning suddenly. "In the tub?"

I smiled, too, and wrapped my arms around his neck. "I'd love to."

He stood, lifting me and then lowered us both into the tub on our sides, facing each other. He let his thumb run a smooth path across my cheek, taking away the wetness there that was pointless to let fall anyway.

He pressed his lips to my forehead and whispered his words against my skin. "Tomorrow, we'll go to The Wall and get this all straightened out. But for tonight, I want you all to myself with no television or brothers or noise. Just you and only you."

"And you," I whispered back.

"And me." I felt his smile, but then he gripped me tighter on my waist and sighed long and loud. "Today was…you could have been… Tomorrow won't be any better. The Wall is worse. I'm trying not to lose it, Clara, but I-"

I kissed his cheek to silence him. "Not tonight, ok? Right now, I just want to feel you."

"You *can* feel me can't you?" He sighed onto my cheek. "The Devourer blood is changing you."

"Maybe," I conceded and snuggled closer. "But the *Devourer* was already changing me."

We silently agreed to let that drop for the night. Instead I asked, "Will the Witch stay that way because of my skin?"

"No. It only lasts a day." He added wryly, "But a Witch can get a lot done in twenty four hours."

I closed my eyes and accepted his gentle caresses and kisses gratefully, loving the feel of him tucking my hair back. Then he pulled the corner of the blanket over us in a not-so-subtle command to sleep.

And I did.

Thirteen

"So when exactly are we going to get up, catch a chartered boat, and get ourselves to Arequipa to The Wall?" Finn said as I rubbed my eyes and peeked over the tub edge. How did he unlock the door? He was still wearing the same clothes as last night. I could also see Enoch leaning over from his perch on the bed to get a good view.

That made me remember what Finn had done. And then the trembling beneath me - Eli's rage - made me remember that Eli and Finn hadn't had their confrontation yet.

"Clara, watch out, sweetheart," he said carefully, not taking his eyes from Finn, as he attempted to ease me to the side to get up. "Stay here so I'm not worried about you getting hurt."

"Now, Eli, come on," Finn said and put his hands up. "I can see you're angry."

"Angry?" Eli whispered as he stepped from the tub. I watched over the rim with fearful anticipation. "You kissed the girl I love." I sucked in a startled, happy breath at his words. He peeked back at me and seemed almost shy as he watched my reaction for a moment. Then he smiled with one side of his mouth before turning back to Finn. "And you tried to overwhelm her with your lust so she'd betray me and I'd hate her. Right? So why would I be angry?" he finished sarcastically.

"But she passed the test," Finn defended vehemently. "I was just looking out for your best interests."

"And in your best interests, I suggest you run," Eli answered and took a step.

"Eli, come on, man."

"Last chance, Finn." He was at the door of the bathroom and Finn was scrambling, bumping into the bed and tripping near the bird cage.

The bird squawked, "Watch out, watch out!"

"Eli-" Finn tried once more, but Eli had reached him.

"Time's up," he said low and dangerously and then reared back with Devourer speed and hit Finn so hard in his jaw that he spun around.

I scrambled up from the tub and ran into the bedroom just in time to see Eli pick Finn up and punch him again. Finn wasn't even fighting back. Eli landed one final blow to Finn's pretty face before grabbing my hand and pulling me out the door. "It's dawn. We're late."

Ah! The stone!

We ran where the Witch said to go. Eli's GPS on his phone said it wasn't far, thank goodness. We got there to find an Elf and a very small man leaning against the phone booth on the sidewalk. They looked peeved.

"Sorry. We got held up," Eli said and held out his hand. "The stone?"

The Elf was smoking again and it was really strong this time, even in the outside air. My throat tickled with a cough, but I tried to hold it back. I inhaled deeply, but that made it worse and I choked on it.

"Can you put that out for two seconds?" Eli barked at him.

The Elf grinned before leaning forward quickly and blowing the smoke directly in our faces. I expected a coughing fit, but what I got was a calm that seemed to settle on me. Eli's shoulders visibly relaxed and I looked at them. He had really nice shoulders. I bit my lip as he held his arm out and the muscles rippled through his shirt. I had to reach out and touch them. So I did.

Eli shuddered when I did and the Elf seemed pleased with himself. "Give him the stone, Barkley. These two look like they want to be alone." He laughed.

The little man plopped the stone in Eli's hand and ran to catch up with the Elf. Eli turned to me and I was engulfed in the flames from his stare. He was on fire from the inside out - I know I sure was - and I could see it in his eyes.

He moved closer and looked down at me. "The smoke," he muttered, trying to grip onto sanity. "The smoke makes you do things-"

I grabbed him around his neck and dragged him down to me. That was the end of any plights for sanity. He lifted me and carried me like that, kissing me and holding me with my legs around him all the way to the hotel. He pressed me to the wall by our room and tried to fish the key out of his pocket, but he couldn't stop kissing me to do it.

And I had no intentions of stopping.

Finally he jiggled the door open and we crashed through it. I heard Enoch muttering a curse, but Eli quickly threw me on the bed and grabbed them both by their shirts to throw them out. Enoch looked at us both and realization dawned. He yelled. "Friggin' Elf smoke! Eli, do what you want, man, but you know you're going to regret it later when the smoke clears." Eli shoved him out the door and started to slam it. "Eli, dude, you know I don't care, but…the bond. You're both going to regret this!"

"Out!" Eli roared before slamming the door, dead bolting it and turning to me. He looked wild, and it fueled me to be not only bold, but brazen. I got up on my knees and beckoned him to me. He plowed into me as gently as our sudden need would allow and I fell back on the bed that I'd just sat up from.

His mouth sucked on my earlobe before moving to my neck. I wrapped myself around him, willing to let all my beliefs slide away. It was unexplainable the way that I just…needed him, right here with me, just like this. My muddled brain said *screw everything else and just let me feel Eli.*

His hand made a slow path from my knee to my hip to my side. His fingers squeezed. A noise I'd never heard before came from my throat. He looked up at my face and watched me. He couldn't seem to stop kissing me though, so with his eyes open, he kissed my lips in soft pecks, over and over. His eyes seemed to focus more as he worked something out in his mind.

I was getting impatient. What was he waiting for?

"Don't stop," I complained.

His eyes snapped open widely at that and he kissed my lips, even as he dragged me from the bed. I clung to him as he carried me and the war waged on his face. He kissed my neck as he climbed into the tub with me. He pressed me to the wall and kissed my open mouth, deep and heady…

Before turning the freezing cold shower on us both.

I gasped, but couldn't seem to stop kissing him. Eventually the cold seeped into me and I started to feel clearer and more level headed. I pulled back from him and saw that he, too, was coming back to himself.

Oh, my... I blushed as I realized that I had been attacking him and letting him attack me...we'd been about to....if Eli hadn't thrown us in the shower...

He tipped my chin and shook his head. "It was the smoke. It was wrangling both of us. Don't feel like that."

"I'm always safe with you, aren't I?" I said as I recognized that he had saved us. I gulped.

"Yes," he answered and kissed me again, but it was just a kiss this time. We sank down to sit in the tub and let the water flow over us. I was cold, but it didn't matter as we sat with our knees up and leaning on each other's. If the cold was what it took to keep a clear head until the smoke was gone, then so be it.

"I think we're ok now," he said, his arm snaking around my shoulders to turn off the water. He sighed and whispered his words, "You trust me still?"

"I trust you more now than ever."

He smiled sadly and helped me up. We toweled off and he went to let them back in the room. I rolled my eyes and cringed as I heard Finn making cracks about me being 'virtueless' now.

I took a deep breath and opened the door to the room. Then I felt something sear through my head, right in the front of my forehead. I gripped it and noticed my hand was blurry. Everything went red...and then everything was black.

~ ~~

It smelled horrible, like feet and bleach. I wrinkled my nose and then heard a loud noise near my ear. I winced and shied away. Hands came up to my face, gentle and soothing. I knew those hands.

"Eli," I said, but my voice croaked. What was wrong with me?

"I'm right here, baby," he said. It sounded like I was talking to him through a window. And he sounded so distraught. I made my eyes open to take in the room. It was too bright and white. Eli immediately jumped up and pulled the string above my bed. The lights dimmed and I blinked to see him better.

"Eli."

"Right here, love," he repeated and smoothed my hair from my forehead with his fingers. He started to smile, but stopped and gawked at me.

"What?"

"Your eyes..." He could see I was about to get frustrated with having to drag it out of him, so he shook his head quickly and continued. "You have one green eye and one purple." He gulped. "Oh, God, please," he said to no one and then laid his head on my stomach.

Ok, maybe he was speaking to someone. I barely heard his words as Eli begged God for my life. He made all kinds of promises and said he loved me over and over and over. I didn't know if God would be listening to a Devourer's prayer or not, but the things Eli was saying... He wasn't asking for me not to die as much as he was asking for me not to be like him.

I touched his hair with my fingers, ignoring the tubes and then gasped as I felt something bury itself in my chest. It stung and barbed into me. It felt too hot, rotten...putrid. And when a startled Eli sat up and I saw the tortured look on his face, I knew exactly what it was. He was feeding me his sorrow and guilt. And I never, ever, ever wanted to feel it again. I understood now. Eli said he hated the way my fear and sorrow tasted. I couldn't taste anything, I even licked my lips to test it, but I could feel it. And it was horrifying.

"Please, stop, Eli. Please," I groaned.

"I'm sorry," he said and ran the backs of his fingers down my cheek, collecting tears. "I'm sorry."

"Where am I?"

"You fainted. I was so scared…I knew what was wrong with you was supernatural, but I couldn't just let you lay there and not do anything. I brought you here. They think you're dehydrated, which may be true, too." He grit his teeth, his jaw hard. "You didn't even eat any supper last night. And we spent all night in the club, dancing and sweating and… I'm not taking very good care of you."

"I'm a big girl, Eli. If I wanted to eat, I would have said something."

"But you didn't say anything because of the smoke. You didn't care about anything last night, you even let that Witch cut a skin sacrifice off of you!" he said vehemently and then closed his eyes as he inhaled a large breath. "I'm sorry. It was my job to take care of you, watch out for you, and so far I'm failing miserably."

I saw his point of view, but I didn't want him to feel bad. I was responsible for myself. "Get me out of here?"

He nodded without hesitation and helped me sit up. I took the glass of ice water on the bedside table and gulped it down. Oh, boy, I was thirsty. I asked him to pour another glass and drank that down, too.

"Slowly," he coaxed. His eyes squinted as he looked away guiltily.

I stood, but swayed a little. His arms snapped out to grip me. "I'm ok," I told him.

"No. You're not," he said sullenly.

He grabbed a hospital bag from under the bed and tossed it on the mattress. Then he put an arm around my waist and the other undid the ties of my hideous hospital gown. He took my sweater and put it gently over my head and shoulders. Then he pulled my gown down and finished the sweater by putting my arms inside.

I felt ok, mostly, just tired and dizzy, but Eli apparently needed to do this for me. To feel like he was taking care of me, so I let him. And I managed not to blush at what he did next, but the doctor walked in just as Eli was letting me step into my skirt. Eli pulled it up and pretended he hadn't seen the doctor, who gawked and started to stutter about me being out of bed.

"I think we're going to go," Eli said looked at him over his shoulder. "And you think it's a good idea, don't you?"

"Um..."

"Yes, it's a good idea," I said and stared at the doctor. He blinked and then nodded slightly as he turned to go.

Eli gazed at me with equal parts wonder and horror. I did that; I made the guy leave with...persuasion. I looked down at my feet. I had hospital slippers on. He lifted my face with his fingers delicately on my neck and jaw. He leaned forward and kissed my forehead. Then he picked me up in his arms under my knees and behind my back.

I didn't have any shoes.

He carried me that way all the way out of the hospital to our hotel room. It was only about five blocks. The sun beat down on us, but it felt heavenly to my tired body. Another headache had begun behind my eyes so I kept my face pressed into his neck until we arrived.

Enoch and Finn were there, and Enoch was pacing. He stopped and stared when Eli entered, but Eli took me straight to the bathroom and closed the door. He turned on the bath water, the steam rising up quickly, and dumped the bottle of hand soap from the sink into it.

When the bubbles started he came to me, all gentle touches and reassuring looks. He rubbed a thumb over my eyebrows and looked at my eyes. My mismatched eyes.

"I won't look," he promised softly and without giving me time to over think, he pulled my shirt over my head. I looked down when he knelt at my feet to remove my hospital slippers. His eyes were closed as he finished undressing me and stood. He held my arm as I lowered myself into the bubbles. I sighed out loud and he took that as his cue to open his eyes.

"Better?"

I nodded. "Much. Thank you."

"We need to get going as soon as you're done," he explained. "We have to take a boat the rest of the way. Are you going to be ok with that?"

The thought of rocking on a boat for hours with this headache made me nauseas, but I nodded my head anyway. He spent the next thirty minutes kneeling on the floor beside the tub watching me. He leaned his head on his arm and took my soapy hand in his, lacing our fingers and massaging my skin.

Eventually he had me lean forward and he washed my hair for me. I told him I was fine to get myself out. He smirked in tolerance and stood, closing his eyes as he held the towel out. When he wrapped it around me, he pulled me to him and hugged me. "Can you do me a favor?"

"Sure. If I can."

"Can you sit here while I take a shower?" He set me on the toilet lid. "I don't want you out there with them alone and I *really* need to shower."

"Ok," I answered and turned my back to the tub. I picked up my hairbrush and tried to get all the tangles out as he started the water again. Within three minutes, he was done and standing behind me in his clean clothes.

He went and got me some clothes out of my bag, but I assured him I was ok to dress myself. He sighed, but let me have it. I dressed quickly and threw my hair into a ponytail. I didn't put on any make-up or earrings. The mirror was not my friend today. She was telling me I had huge bags under my eyes and bruises on my arms from the IVs, and a large bandage - that the hospital must have replaced - covering my skin sacrifice. And the durable band-aid had survived the bath.

I licked my dry lips, so confused as to why I was dying of thirst again. I opened the door and, surprisingly, Enoch was first to jump up and make his way to me. He stopped, his eyes wide and angry.

"Now what?" he roared and looked at Eli accusingly. "What's going on?"

"I don't know," Eli said in defeat.

Enoch looked back to me. "Do you feel different?"

"Yes," I answered truthfully. "I feel like..." I thought about how to word it and the description that came was too eerie and appropriate. "Like I'm being ripped in two different directions."

"That's because you are," Eli said and came to me. "The Devourer and human blood are fighting for dominancy."

Finn was on the far corner of the bed, watching us. Enoch looked at me with displeasure, probably because he'd been worried about me through the bond and he hated to feel anything for me. And Eli was focused on nothing but me. "I'm ready to go when you are," I told him

"I'll never be ready for this," he said quietly. He pulled out his phone and mumbled about it being dead, then picked up the hotel phone. "Yeah, I need a cab, please."

"Why?" Enoch asked while Eli talked to the cab company. "Why do you have Devourer blood? The bond shouldn't have anything to do with that."

"I..." I didn't really want to tell him that I'd licked Eli's blood before. "I put Eli's blood in me." His eyes widened. "It was an accident."

"So...you're turning into a Devourer?" He grinned. "You're not going to be a filthy feeler anymore?"

"Thanks, Enoch," I said dryly and went to go sit on the bed. He grabbed my arm to help me. I looked at him curiously. "Why are you helping me?"

"Don't read too much into it," he replied and smirked. "But I have no problems being family if you're a Devourer. So as soon as all that feeler blood is out of your system, you and I will be all good."

"It's killing her!" Eli boomed and threw the hotel phone across the room. It smashed into the wall, but he didn't care as he glared at Enoch. "Don't make this a joke! It's not. It's killing her, not changing her."

"How do you know that?" Enoch scoffed.

"Because you can't be made into a Devourer. You're born one or you're not."

"Whatever. I think that Finn's right. If she's unbound, then you won't care so much anymore-"

Eli went to him, nose to nose. "Don't." He took a deep breath. "You two stay here. We'll go."

"Not a chance," Enoch refuted. "I'm not leaving her side until she's either a Devourer or unbound or..." he narrowed his eyes, "not breathing. I can't live with the nagging bond always calling me to her."

"Then you keep your lovely comments to yourself," Eli growled.

"Comments to yourself!" Cavuto squawked. "Raaayk!"

"The last thing she needs is to worry about you two," Eli continued.

He pushed passed him and grabbed my bag off the bed. My flip-flops were on top and he laid them at my feet. I slipped them on and didn't say anything to anyone as he grabbed the bird's cage with my bag over his shoulder. He gripped my hand and walked with me out the door, not even looking back to see if they were coming.

Fourteen

The boat they chartered was small. I gulped as we stepped on board and Eli situated me on a leather bench. He paid the man and Finn just couldn't resist, thin ice be darned.

"Why pay him at all?" he sneered and plopped on the bench across from us. "Just persuade him to take us!"

"I don't do that anymore. I have the money."

"So do I, but that doesn't mean that you can't get a free ride once in a while. Two thousand bucks is a hefty price for a joyride across the water."

Eli looked at me. "I'm not that man anymore."

Finn shook his head and closed his eyes as he sang, "Kumbaya, my Lord! Kumbaya!" Enoch burst out laughing. Finn opened his eyes to see us glaring at him. "What? I thought we were having an open heart moment."

"Bite me, Finn," Eli said and I caught his small smile he tried to hide.

In reality, from a girl's point of view, yes, Finn was a douche bag. But from the guy's point of view - the best friend's point of view - he was trying to help him I guessed. If I was truly was bonded and committed to him, then I shouldn't have really been affected by Finn. I got it. I didn't like him, but I got it.

"What now?" I asked Eli and put my aching head on his shoulder.

"Straight to The Wall," he explained. "I'm not wasting a minute."

Finn rolled his eyes, and then my phone rang. I jolted and grabbed it from my bag. We'd be out to sea soon and it wouldn't work anymore. I saw I had a couple of texts from Ariel and Mrs. Ruth was calling.

"Hi," I said and tried to sound chipper.

"Clara, hi, honey. How's everything going?"

"Good. What's up?"

"Well…" she stalled. "I just…I know we let you go, and in my mind it seems like a good idea, but I honestly have no idea why. I have no idea why we would think it was a good idea for you to go off somewhere with your boyfriend. It has me worried. Not about you," she said hurriedly, "just worried...in general."

"Well, we needed to do some things, Mrs. Ruth," I said and watched Eli as I spoke. His interest was piqued. He looked confused. "I'll be back soon, and I'm glad you trust me enough to go."

"That's the thing, Clara. I don't." I sat, stunned. "It's not that I don't trust you, or Eli, I just don't trust you alone together. You're very different with him than you were with Tate. More…serious. You love him, I can see it. That's why I'm so confused as to why I'm all right with you being gone with him."

What could I say to that? "I'm sorry. I'll be home soon, ok? How is everyone?"

"Oh, we're fine," she said happily, almost as if the rest was forgotten. "The kids are all taking naps at the same time now, thank the Lord. Pastor's been worried about you, though. He was a little upset that I let you leave, but I assured him you'd be back soon and that it was ok."

"Thank you, Mrs. Ruth." I sighed. "I miss you."

"It's only been a day, Clara."

I nodded, though she couldn't see me. "Yeah, but it feels like an eternity."

"You'll be home tomorrow, right?"

"I'll try."

"Ok, well if you get a chance, call Pastor tonight. He'd love to hear it for himself."

"Ok," I said, but knew I wasn't going to do that. "I love you, Mrs. Ruth."

I realized that I'd never said that to her before. I heard her soft gasp before she said, "I love you, too, honey. You're sure you're all right?"

"Yes, ma'am."

"Ok," she said reluctantly. "I'll see you tomorrow then."

"Bye," I said and let the phone drop from my fingers into the pocket on my bag.

"I guess my persuasion wasn't up to par, huh?" Eli said dryly. "Sorry."

"It's ok," I said truthfully and lay down, putting my head in his lap. "What about the Horde?"

"What about them?"

"The Witch who gave you the stone had to know where we were going. She said she'd give us a head start. You're not afraid the Horde will be there waiting for us?"

"They might be," he agreed, "but it's worth the risk to get you better."

"Dead is better?" Enoch muttered and I looked at him. He pointed angrily to his bond and screwed up his lips. "Bond! I don't give a flip, but the frigging bond is pissed you're even thinking about it now that the Witch is on to you."

"Has to be done," Eli said, his eyes closed as he leaned his head back. His fingers combed through my hair and I wanted to groan at how good it felt against my pounding head. "I'll keep her safe, but The Wall is the only place to get the answers. Once we're in, the Horde can't touch us until we come back out again."

"Why?" I ask distractedly.

"Because the Horde doesn't go to The Wall. They think it's betrayal and disgusting to mix and mingle the races that way. Just like Consumed Clubs. They don't go against them, but they avoid them."

"I just can't wait to get there," Finn said dreamily. "There're so many Sirens!" He grinned. "Do you have any idea what feeding emotion from a Siren is like?" He shivered in delight. I almost vomited in disgust.

"This is about you getting your kicks with Sirens? I thought you wanted the bond broken?" Eli asked.

"Oh, I do. And I'm pretty confident that we can do that. But who says we can't have a little fun, too?"

"I think you should sell the bird, Eli," Enoch said, eying the creature. "He's no use to you and I bet you could get a good price for him."

"I'm not sure that's a good idea," Eli said. "I feel like he's got a secret that that I haven't figured out yet."

"How poetic," Finn muttered.

The bird held itself against the side of the cage and yelled, "Arequipa! Arequipa!"

"We're going!" Finn yelled and gave Eli a strange look. "How can you stand that thing?"

"I don't know. It definitely does *not* grow on you."

"A Goblin's tooth is all you need!" Cavuto yelled.

"What's he going on about?" Enoch asked.

"We don't know," Eli answered and sat up a bit. "He keeps saying it."

"Arequipa!"

"Shut it, bird!" Finn said and shook the cage with his foot, causing the bird to shriek and squawk.

"Hey," I said and wondered why I needed to defend the bird who hated me, but I just did. "It's a bird. What do you want us to do? Muzzle it?"

"We could muzzle you," he rebutted and smiled. "I'd pay a thousand bucks to see it done."

"Finn," Eli warned. Finn rolled his purple eyes and muttered something about making a phone call before we got too far from shore.

"Do you feel all right?" Enoch asked me, surprising me and Eli.

"Yes. Why?"

"Because the bond is going nuts right now." He rubbed his wrist. "Really it's been going nuts for days. It doesn't make any sense."

"It makes perfect sense," Eli said sadly. "The bond is letting you know that the Devourer blood is hurting her."

"But...I feel fine right now," I said. "I don't feel any different."

"It's ok," Eli soothed and pulled me back down to lay on him. My stomach growled loudly and I peeked up to see Eli laughing silently.

"It was that loud, huh?" I said and felt myself blushing a little.

"It's like your body is trying to eat itself," Enoch muttered in disgust. "I'll ask the Captain what he's got to eat. There better be a meal included for what Eli paid."

"I'm sorry," Eli said suddenly. "I should have made sure you ate before we left shore." He sighed. "There I go again, being really crappy at taking care of you."

"It's ok, Eli. We've been a little preoccupied."

"That's no excuse."

Enoch came back and said the Captain, i.e. a small Guatemalan man who barely spoke a lick of English, said that dinner would be served in a half hour. My stomach growled happily at the news. Little did I know that 'dinner being served' meant egg salad sandwiches and a bag of Cheetos to share.

I scarfed the meal; the pickle bits stuck in the egg salad seemed to hit the spot perfectly. I drank all of my Dr Pepper and then grabbed the bag of Cheetos from Enoch to take with me.

"Hey!" Enoch complained as his hand was yanked out of it.

"I'm the only one on this boat who *has* to eat except the Captain. Bite me."

"Don't tempt me," he growled.

I went to the bow and leaned against the rail as I munched on the cheesy goodness. Cheetos were practically the best invention ever.

Eli chuckled as he came up behind me and caged me with his arms against the rail. It reminded me of our date at the club with Patrick. It seemed forever ago. "Cheeto thief."

"Guilty," I said and popped another one in my mouth. "Mrs. Ruth never has crunchy Cheetos in the house because she read in a parenting magazine that they're a choking hazard."

"So you're getting your fill," he said amused and reached around me to steal a few. I heard his crunch in my ear. "Best invention ever."

I turned to him in surprise. "I literally just thought that exact thing like ten seconds ago."

"So surprised?" he smiled. "Didn't you know we were perfect for each other?"

I smiled and nodded. "I did know that."

"Good. You look so much better," he observed. "And you seem in higher spirits."

"Talking to Mrs. Ruth was good." I thought about it. "I never really embraced her as a mother figure, and I realized that when she called. It's like I've been subconsciously waiting for my mom to come back. But she's not, and I need to move on. Pastor and Ruth love me. I thought when I moved in that I'd be just be a burden or a guest, but *I* made myself that way."

"And now?"

"Now, they're my family and it's time I start acting like it."

He toyed with his tongue ring with his teeth, his eyes unfocused. "Can I ask you something?"

"Mmhmm," I mumbled and popped another Cheeto.

"The truth. Do you want kids someday?"

I stopped and stared at him. "Can I be truthful and you not try to put some on self-deprecating act?"

He laughed in surprise. "Sure, yes."

"I'm not sure." The answer surprised him. "I think I would, but…things have changed."

"Because of me?" he said and screwed up his lips.

"That sounds like self-deprecation," I sang.

"Am I the reason?" he insisted.

"If we had kids," I hedged, "would they be Devourers?"

"No," he answered softly.

"Then why was Hatch going on about-"

"He thinks it's wrong, an abomination. But Devourers can't be made; they have to be born of two Devourers. If we had children, they wouldn't be different than any other human child. They'd never feel different, or act or look or know different."

I licked my lips. "Yes, I want kids one day. Can I ask you a question?"

"Of course."

I held my breath as I asked, "Why did you ask me about children?"

He looked at me closely, and I knew he was looking at my mismatched eyes and our possibly broken future, but I didn't look away. "Because I think it's proper to know if the girl I'm in love with wants children someday or not."

My heart stopped. He said it. He said it to me, to my face, with no inflection or deflection.

"I have other questions, too," he continued when I stayed silent. "Where do we want to live after we graduate? What's your favorite restaurant? Do you want to go to college? Do you-"

I cut off his questions with a hug. He sighed and I thought I felt him chuckle, too. "Eli," I said, but it croaked out of me.

He leaned back and the horrified expression on his face told me the tears that were clinging had let go. "Oh, love, I didn't mean to upset you. You don't have to say it back to me. That's not why I-"

"No, dummy, they're tears of happiness," I said. I'd said that to him before when he thought I was upset about the bond. I wasn't upset then and I definitely wasn't upset now.

He remembered and smiled as he repeated what he'd said that day, too, "Then, I'm honored."

"I've never told anyone I loved them before," I explained.

"You don't have to-" he started.

"Eli, shut up," I said softly. He smirked and nodded for me to go on. "I've never said it because I've never felt it and I won't say anything that I don't feel. And I won't say 'I love you, too' because my feelings should be my own, based on what I feel. But you can trust me when I say that...I love you."

His eyelids fluttered a bit before closing. "The best kind of agony," he muttered.

"What do you mean?" I asked and put myself flush to him.

He accepted me into his arms and pressed his forehead to mine. "My heart hurts with the knowledge that I don't deserve you."

"Eli-" I started to argue.

"Clara, shut up," he whispered softly and smiled. I smiled, too, and sighed as a sign to him to keep going. "I don't deserve you and never will, but I'll never let you go." Then he mouthed, "I. Love. You."

I mouthed back, "I. Love. You."

His mouth moved to mine with infinite slowness and torture. Just as his lips touched me, I felt the Cheetos bag fall from my fingers. His lips were warm and soft and damp from where he'd licked them. I sighed when I felt his arm across my back, pulling me up gently. I felt something else, too; a fire in my chest, but the warmth was welcomed.

So...this was what love *felt* like...

I let my hands do what they pleased, and they gripped his neck and hair. He groaned. Hmm. He must like that.

"What...Clara!" Enoch boomed, jolting us to look at him. "You wasted the Cheetos!"

I looked down at my feet to the see the bag of Cheetos leaning over the edge. Eli and I leaned over the boat side to see a sea of orange twigs in our wake. I pressed my lips together. Eli held up his hand to stop it. It didn't help.

We both broke out, bursting in laughter. The kind where you fall on each other to keep from tipping over. The kind where you grip each other and squint eyes and your body threatens to pee on itself if you don't stop. The kind where your future brother-in-laws stomp off in a hissy fit.

The kind that I so desperately needed.

Fifteen

Enoch sulked in the corner chair of the front deck. I tried not to smile about it anymore, though I was thoroughly enjoying the situation at his expense. Eli left me snuggling warmly under a blanket on the bench. He went to speak to the Captain about where exactly he planned to dock. We still had to either do a cab or rent a car to get to The Wall and he was trying to calculate everything.

"You know he only told you he loves you because he thinks you're going to die."

I stilled. Such hatred, such malice, such belligerence from someone who didn't even know me. "Don't talk to me anymore, Finn. I don't want to hear it."

I lay down and pulled the blanket higher.

"I'm just trying to save you some heartache." He shrugged. "You never saw them together, him and Angelina. I don't know what he's told you about them, but she was very much in love with him," he growled and sneered. I looked at him curiously.

"You sound very jealous," I whispered.

He stood and threw his glass on the floor. It shattered, but before the glass even flitted its way across the deck, Enoch was there. He shoved Finn back into his seat and held his hand out in front of me as he spoke to Finn. "I suggest you stop feeling sorry for yourself and shut up."

"Sorry for myself?" he scoffed and glared at me. "And I am not jealous."

"Ok," I said to placate the situation.

He stalked off to the other side of the boat and I sighed as I sat.

"I should never have brought him," Enoch muttered and tossled his hair.

"You brought him to get rid of me," I said softly, but honestly. "Why are you upset that that's exactly what he's trying to do?"

"Because it hurts you to do it," he answered and looked back at me. "The kind of pain and hurt I get through the bond isn't the kind I get when I feed from people. It hurts me to hurt you, or watch you be hurt. Like right now, you're hurting somewhere, aren't you?"

I hesitated and nodded. "My head. It's killing me."

He left without another word and went below. He came back quickly with a glass of ice water and a couple of pills. He held his hand out for me to take them, so I did. "Take it," he ordered quietly. "You should feel better soon."

"Not to jinx anything, but this is the nicest you've ever been to me. Why? I'm not going to be a Devourer, Enoch. I want you to know that so you don't get even more upset later when we fix what's wrong with me."

"Yeah, I figured." He smirked. "High hopes."

"Why?" I repeated.

"Because...I guess I'm stuck with you. And like I said, if hurts when you're hurting. So, self-preservation and all that."

I smiled and nodded. "Right." I took the pills and drank the whole glass of water. Enoch watched me do it, to make sure I was taking them I guess. "I wish Eli and I could feel each other through the bond the way you can me."

"I would gladly offer it to him."

"Why can't your parents feel it?"

"It's a brotherly\sisterly bond thing," he said and waved his hand at me in annoyance.

"Hey, I am sorry, you know."

"For what, princess?" he said snidely. "Ruining my life or making me soft?"

"Both. I would never have bound myself to Eli had I known what would happen to you."

He smiled humorlessly. "Yes, you would have."

I pressed my lips together. "Maybe," I conceded after a pause. "I love him. Like really down-in-my-soul love him. Don't you want to be happy for him?"

"Are you kidding?" he hissed. "You ruined his life before you ruined mine."

"I think your dictionaries are different, Enoch," I said and leaned my head back. It wasn't hurting anymore, but I was so, so tired.

"Hey," Eli asked as he emerged. "What's all the hissing about?" He stepped on the broken glass and it crunched under his feet. "What's this? What happened?" he asked and came to me.

Enoch answered, "She didn't like Finn's advice, and Finn didn't like her assessment of him."

"Assessment?" Eli asked, his brow rose. "What happened?"

"He threw his glass," I said. "He's sulking over there." I waved my hand towards that end of the boat. "He's fine. I'm fine."

"And the hissing?" Eli questioned Enoch.

"No hissing, brother mine. We're just one big happy family."

Eli rolled his eyes and looked to me for the answer. I grinned. He rolled his eyes again and smiled before leaning back on the seat beside me. But then his face changed and he sat back up. He took my chin in his hands and looked at me closely. "Clara, did you take something?"

"Yes, why?"

"Your pupils are dilated," he murmured. "What did you take?" I looked to Enoch in answer. Eli knew immediately what happened and growled as he stood. "What did you give her, Enoch?"

"Just some tranquilizers the old man had stashed in the bathroom."

"Some! Some tranquilizers, as in more than one!" Eli boomed.

"Two. Two will be enough to knock her skinny butt out for a few hours so me and my bond can have some peace and quiet," Enoch said rationally and leaned his head back against the boat side.

Eli was in front of me then. I could hear them, but really, I didn't care. I was just tired. "Can you hear me, love?"

"I hear you. I'm just tired."

He cursed and looked over his shoulder. "Enoch!" he said his name like it was a curse itself.

"I'm trying to rest," Enoch muttered. "Pipe down."

"That's it," Eli said to me. "We'll ditch them in the morning. I can't kill him, but we can leave him."

"Whatever," I muttered. "Lay with me?"

He sighed and cracked his neck like he was exhausted. He scooted me over so he had room and climbed on the bench beside me. He was so warm against the cold wind that I groaned loudly making him chuckle. "Better?"

"Much better."

He pushed my hair back. "I'm sorry."

"It's all right. It's just payback," I muttered. "I'm ok. I needed to sleep anyway."

"Where's my snarky girl?" he said through a chuckle, but it was laced with strain.

"Bite me, Thames," I whispered, making him laugh again.

"Well, there's that." He pressed a sweet kiss to my forehead. "I'll be here all night. I won't leave you for a second."

"I'm not worried."

He scoffed. "Of course you're not. You're high," he added dryly.

"Not high, just tired." I let my fingers tangle in the hair at the nape of his neck. "I love you."

He sighed. "I love you, CB. Go to sleep, baby."

~ ~ ~

My head was splitting, and I was freezing. I shivered and felt hands rubbing my arms. "Sorry. It's really cold at night."

He said something over his shoulder to someone and I felt another blanket land roughly on top of us. Eli grumbled as he spread it out and pulled me closer.

"Where are we?" I murmured.

"Almost there." He kissed my forehead. "Go back to sleep."

"Will you take me somewhere in a reverie?"

"To sleep?" he asked surprised.

"I want you to take me somewhere warm."

I'd barely said the words before I felt the sun on my face. I peeked up to see him sprawled on his side against me on a large beach towel in the sand. The beach was empty of people. I could hear the birds and waves pounding behind us.

"Thank you."

"Anytime, love."

And I fell back to sleep thinking of doing this with Eli for real one day.

~ ~ ~

The rocking boat woke me. I felt nauseas all of a sudden. No, not nauseas. I was upchucking. I scrambled up, leaning over the rail in milliseconds of being too late. But nothing.

My body racked and heaved, but nothing came up. I felt Eli's hand on my back, but I hurt so bad that I couldn't even focus. The blue water beneath me moved and swirled, making my vision blur.

"Ah," I groaned. "I want to just throw up."

"You want to throw up?" Enoch mocked. "Stupid feelers and their strange rituals."

I heard a scuffle and then Eli yelled. "She wants to throw up so she'll feel better, because you drugged her you jackass!" I heard another scuffle, and then a thud before Eli was at my back again. "Love, you ok?"

"Just kill me," I groaned. "Just make it quick," I joked.

"No talk of that," Eli barked, not appreciating my joke. "Come on," he said softer, as he turned me. "You want to freshen up before we go?"

I looked up and saw we were docked. "Arequipa?" I asked.

"Soon. We need to go catch our ride."

"Ok," I said and swallowed to make sure I was going to keep the contents of my stomach for good.

He showed me where the bathroom was, and I brushed my teeth and changed my clothes to some jeans and a layered t-shirt. I let my hair out of its ponytail. It fell in waves. More waves that made me ache even more for my mom. I took a deep breath. Mrs. Ruth has waves, too...

I shook my head and opened the door. Eli was there and took my bag from me. He led me to the top and the Captain threw the plank down for us to walk and cross to the dock.

"All right," Eli said once we all got across. "See ya." He nodded his head to Enoch and Finn, taking my hand and pulling me along the sidewalk.

"Whoa, wait," Finn said frantically. "What are you doing?"

"Neither one of you has Clara's or my interest in mind. You're here for yourselves and we've got enough to deal with than having to worry about your next move on Clara." He pinned Finn with a glare. "You kissing her again," then his glower swung to Enoch, "or you drugging her."

"It told you it was a test-" Finn said while Enoch yelled, "I just wanted her to nap a bit!"

"Whatever! We're done. We're going this way," Eli pointed with my bag in his hand, "and you go that way. So help me...if you follow us..."

His guttural growl even had Enoch looking surprised. Eli pulled me along as he cut through a busy alley full of people. There were fishing boats lining the pier and tables of goods set up. People yelled out to us to come and taste their fish, the freshest in the market they said.

"I'm sorry," I said and gave him a sideline glance.

"Why are you sorry?" he asked. "You didn't tranquilize yourself."

"I'm sorry you had to choose. Them...or me."

"I'll always choose you," he said incredulously.

"And I'll always be sorry that you have to. The jerk is your brother, and the bigger jerk is your best friend."

His brow bunched and he seemed to wonder what to say to that. "Yes, and as such, they should respect my decision."

"Is that something Devourers do? Respect?"

He swallowed and looked uncomfortable. "No."

"Then how can you expect them to?" I said softly. "I'm not saying what they did was right, but they only know one way to live."

"But it doesn't make it ok for them to treat you that way. I can't do anything to stop them because they're immortal. Leaving is the only option."

"I know," I agreed. "I just wanted to make sure you understood all the variables. I don't want you to think one day that you wish you'd tried harder to make it ok with your brother."

"My brother is just another Devourer. We don't view family like that, I told you."

"Then why do you care so much?" I said quietly and touched his cheek. He seemed a little peeved at my ability to see the truth.

"I care, he doesn't. He can't. I just want you."

"But what if I'm not enough one day?"

"Enough for what?" he asked, but kept going as I opened my mouth to speak. "I don't know if you know this, Miss Hopkins, but you are an extreme handful."

I laughed and shook my head in mock anger. "I see."

"I love you. I love everything about you, every inch. I have no doubt that you can keep me occupied and...happy."

"Really? Even if we wind up back in Big Timber with four point five kids, a scraggily dog in the white fenced yard, and living off of a teacher's salary?"

"You want to be a teacher?" he asked distractedly.

"No!" I grimaced. "I meant you. What else are you gonna do other than teach? The high school art teacher can't live forever."

He chuckled reluctantly. And then said, "If that happens, I'll be happy if you are."

"Really?"

"Yes, really," he mocked and smiled as he bumped my shoulder with his. "Your lack of confidence in my ability to not only provide for you, but be entertaining enough to keep you happy is a little disconcerting."

I just smiled as I let him lead me and put my head on his shoulder.

The fish market was pretty smelly to say the least, but the bead merchant's tables were beautiful. I didn't know if Eli caught me eying them or just decided on his own, but he pulled me to one of the tables and started to pick through them.

He held up one that was green, grey and blue and slipped it around my wrist. He tilted his head to the side to get a good look and then asked her how much. The number was practically nothing. He forked over the money and tipped his head to her as we went. She was so grateful as she bowed and said her thanks in words I didn't understand. It hit me how some people were dependent on so little and worked their whole lives just to make ends meet.

It put things into terrible perspective.

Eli hailed a cab - an old Range Rover that had seen better days - throwing our stuff in the back and setting the bird in the front seat. I found it odd that the driver didn't act as though this was uncommon; for animals to ride shotgun.

"Arequipa!" the bird screeched.

"Yes, Cavuto. Arequipa," Eli agreed.

Sixteen

"Are we close?" I whispered anxiously.

He squeezed my hand, his thumb rubbing over the wrist. "Kind of, sort of…not really."

I scowled causing him to laugh. "You want to explain?"

"Nah," he whispered through a chuckle, and then explained quietly in my ear. "The Wall moves. It not a place, it's a plane. I can find it, but that's why we needed the Witch's stone. You can't get in without it."

"So…how will you find it?"

"I just will," he said cryptically. He reached over and palmed my cheek gently. "How are you feeling?"

"I'm ok," I said, but the headache was back. I covered his hand with mine and closed my eyes. The cab suddenly stopped and he turned to us.

"This is the last town for a long time. If you need to use the lavatories, you'd better."

"Food," Eli said and pulled me from the side door.

~ ~ ~

After he purchased a couple of sandwiches, with meat that I was scared to ask the origin of, we made our way back to the cab. He bumped us down the rough, unkempt roads as we ate and Eli tried to calm me with stories of his travels. He'd been to almost every country there was, every continent, heard every tongue spoken. I was awed and enraptured as I chewed and listened.

He was saying something about how Canadians were the most docile people he'd ever encountered when the pain in my head exploded. The bright light was there again, blocking my vision and blinding me painfully. The sandwich fell from my fingers and I rubbed my face in an effort to help. It didn't.

I heard Eli's muffled, "Love?" but the ringing in my ears was too loud. I scratched at my arms as they pulsed painfully and felt as if they'd rip open. Then everything went black again.

~ ~ ~

I was being lifted. I could hear shouting. Enoch? Finn? Eli's warm arms were around me and then we were running. I heard Cavuto squawking angrily and assumed he was being jostled in his cage.

I hurt. I hurt all over, a stinging, burning kind of pain. My arms and head hurt the worst. I tried to peel my eyes open…Eli?

He was tortured. His face a mask of anger, self-hate and worry. I reached up to soothe him by touching his cheek, but before my arm got there I saw it. My veins…were blue and protruding.

I looked up at Eli in a silent question, but he stopped and jerked us into the woods. He said something to Enoch and Finn and waited, then pulled my shirt over my head. I was too shocked to do anything but let him. He rummaged through my bag until he found what he was looking for and pulled the red long sleeve sweater over my head, fixing it on my body.

He smoothed the sleeves down, his thumbs rubbing the veins delicately like they would burst at any moment. "Stay with me, Clara," he whispered and I heard him. "Please."

"I'm right here," I whispered back and he jolted.

He said something louder, my name I think, but it was muffled again. I winced. "Clara?" he whispered in anguish.

"That's it," I whispered. "Whisper. It's too loud and I can't understand you otherwise."

"Ok," he whispered back. "We're here. We're at The Wall."

I opened my eyes again, but the sun was so bright, I felt like it was burning them. I made a noise of protest. Eli yelled something behind him and then set a pair of sunglasses on my face gently. I peeked my eyes open again, and it was much better.

"Better?" he said softly. I nodded. He cocked his head to the side thinking and then grabbed the shirt I'd just taken off and ripped a piece of the sleeve off. My mouth opened in protest, but he just closed it with easy fingers.

He whispered, "I'm performing a little experiment, CB, and your shirt is a sacrifice for that."

"But it's my Spirit squad shirt," I complained.

He grinned then and ripped the small piece into two before pinching and balling them up, placing them in my ears.

"How's that?" he said normally and I couldn't help but sigh in relief.

Then Eli glared at Finn. "You stole my sunglasses?" Finn just shrugged and lifted a brow like why should Eli be surprised. Eli looked back at me. "Your senses are all screwy." He sighed and ran a trembling hand through his hair. "Do you think you can walk?"

"Honestly? I don't want to," I answered.

"I'm sorry, love, but you have to. I can't carry you into The Wall. You have to go of your own free will."

"Are we here?" I said and looked around.

He nodded and looked at me in sympathy. "Baby steps. Can you stand?"

I could try. So I accepted his hand and let him lift me up. I was wobbly, but standing. I pushed up my sleeve and rubbed at the veins on my forearm. He pushed the sleeve down and mouthed, "Don't."

"It's getting worse," I stated the obvious.

"Yeah," he sighed. "Come on, love, I can't wait anymore to get you fixed."

He wrapped his arm around my waist and I let my arm drape around his shoulder. He went slowly out of the woods and towards a small pond. The barbed string hung around his chest down to his arm and I wondered what we were going to do about hiding it this time. So I asked him.

"Eli. The string."

"People at The Wall don't care as much. They mind their own business, but just keep your hand in mine and hopefully, we won't have to wonder if they care that much or not."

"Pretty flimsy risk taking," Enoch muttered.

"How are they here?" I whispered.

"They followed us," he grumbled and kissed my forehead and spoke against my skin in a soothing manner. "Don't worry. I've got my eyes on them."

He stopped at the bank of the lake. He reached into his pocket, while keeping his other arm around me, and pulled out the stone. His fingers turned it over and over for a few moments and then he chucked it into the water.

We waited.

"Did you stash our bags?" Eli said someone without looking back at them.

"Yeah," Finn answered.

I looked at Eli in question. "We can't take anything with us," he explained. "Enoch, will you let Cavuto out?"

"You're not leaving him here with your stuff?" he asked.

"No."

I heard the cage door rattling and then Cavuto flew and landed on Eli's shoulder. "Arequipa!"

"Yes, Cavuto," Eli murmured and then the water started to boil.

I watched as the water churned and bubbled, the sun glinting off the peaks making it seem every bit of ethereal and magical. Ke$ha's "Blow" was playing through my mind for some reason. It was scary how appropriate it fit, but I didn't even like that song.

A stone pathway appeared from below the surface. "Finn, will you go first so Cavuto has someone to go to?" Eli asked.

Finn huffed in an exaggerated way and made his way from the bank to the stones. He crossed swiftly. He reached the last one and I held my breath as he jumped and…vanished into the water below.

There was no splash.

I gulped. Eli pulled my face to look at him. "It's all right. It's a plane, remember? You can't think with your eyes here. I promise you it'll be ok. Cavuto, go."

He did, stepping and hopping from one stone to the next and then jumping up just as Finn had and disappearing.

"Why does the bird have to go like that?" I asked in a whisper.

"He has to go of his own free will just like the rest of us."

Enoch followed Cavuto. I could hear him muttering something as it echoed against the water. "Third star to the right and straight on 'til morning." He jumped from the last stone, yelling "Olly, olly, oxen free!" and plunged soundlessly into the water.

Eli turned to me. "You're next, don't argue. I threw the stone, I have to close it by going last." He kissed my lips, lingering, and then leaned his head against mine. "I wish I could carry you or help, but… It's daytime here, but it's always dark there so be careful when you step out. I'll be right behind you," he promised, his voice low and gravelly.

I took a tentative step and though my legs shook, I could keep myself upright. I stepped on the first stone and determined it was solid. I went on slowly and when I reached the last one I swallowed hard, knowing this was the definition of a leap of faith. The water looked normal below me, but I knew it wasn't and I knew it would carry me to another place.

You can't think with your eyes here, Eli had said. I closed them and without waiting to over think, I jumped with both feet straight out below me.

Seventeen

I landed with my feet firmly planted on the hard ground below me, but teetered and tipped forward with the momentum. I held my hands out to catch myself from the hard ground, but instead got a hard chest. I peeked my eyes open to find Enoch with his arms around me, my nose pressed into his shirt. I jerked back and almost fell again.

He growled and gripped me tighter. "Will you just wait for Captain Bleeding Heart before you hurt yourself? I'm not going to bite you."

"I've got her," Eli said from behind me and pulled me to him. I looked around over his shoulder. The sky was pitch black, not a star in sight. It didn't remind me of a beautiful night sky to watch and lay under, it looked empty and evil. He leaned back to look at me. "You good?"

"Yeah." I looked back at Enoch. "Thanks."

"I didn't want you to smash that pretty face," he sneered.

"Aw, you think I'm pretty?" I said smartly, causing him to glare at me.

"All right," Eli said, always the moderator. "Cavuto, come on."

The bird flew to his shoulder once more and Eli looked around as if looking for something specific. Then he pulled my hand for me to follow him. There was a large stone and stucco wall, and he searched for something along the surface. There was a sliver of light and Eli gripped the edges of the opening quickly with both hands. He pulled and the sliver opened further. It groaned and complained under his strain. Eli's face was red and shaking as he moved his head for us to go through as he held it. Enoch pushed me forward with hands on my back as we ducked under Eli's arm. Once we were through, Eli bolted through and turned back to watch the wall close with a groan.

We were in an alley of some sort. He gripped my hand tightly and gave me a hard look. "You can't be human here. You can't be smart mouthed. You can't show that you're sick right now and you can't, under any circumstances, leave my side. Understand?"

"Yes," I said and that was all. I knew this was serious and he was worried that I was going to cause trouble. Kind of like I almost did at the Consumed Club. I grumbled at myself.

"Ok," he softer and lowered his voice. "Remember, if I treat you different here, it's because I have to. Let's just find what we need and get out of here and go home, ok?"

"You had me at get out of here and go home."

He smiled. "Good girl." He turned. "Finn- Where's Finn?"

Enoch shrugged. "He was already gone when I came through." Then his face hardened and he looked at me before settling back on Eli. They stared at each other with a silent understanding. "Something smells fishy and it ain't the Sushi Bar."

"Finn was always out for himself," Eli pondered and bit at his tongue ring. "Maybe he just used us to get a stone so he could come in?"

"Doubtful." Enoch moved closer. "What if it has to do with the Horde?"

"He wouldn't..." Eli's face fell. "He wouldn't."

"Let's go, Eli. Let's find the Soothsayer and go."

"Soothsayer?" I asked.

"Like a...fortune teller or oracle," Eli said distractedly. "She's the only one who can tell us how to fix you."

We started walking without another word. Enoch flanked me on my other side and it was as unnerving as it was comforting. We emerged from the alley, and I gasped silently at the amount of people there. It was a market, tables everywhere, people yelling and haggling over prices. Creatures, some I recognized from the club, some not, were scattered in every direction. They offered us things as we moved through the throngs.

A tall older woman offered me a cup of something green. My tongue was suddenly dryer than the Sahara and I reached for it without thinking. Enoch grabbed my arm just before reaching it and gave Eli a look. Eli pulled my arm and put me against his side. "You can't take things from people here."

"Why not? I'm thirsty."

"Because if you thought the Elf smoke was bad, that will take you to the moon, Clara."

"It's drugged?" I said conspiratorially.

"No. It *is* a drug. Don't eat or drink anything here."

I nodded. We pushed on through the people and I tried not to focus on any one thing or person. It smelled horrible with all the mixed scents of food and spices and smokes. My sense of smell must have been whacked up, too.

Eli pulled us to a little door and knocked - no lie- fourteen times. A peek hole opened up high and then closed. Another peek hole opened lower and then closed. The door opened, but there was no one there to usher us in. I gripped Eli's hand tightly and tried not to think or feel. Just breathe.

Eli pulled us through a hallway and knocked on another door. "I need to see Anastasia."

"What fer?" an annoyed voice barked. "She ain't in need a no company!"

Eli cursed softly and then gave me a grave look. He implored me with his eyes, but I didn't understand why. He said loudly as he stared into my eyes, "I need to offer her a proposition."

"In exchange for what?"

"The whereabouts of the Soothsayer, Magenta."

The door creaked open and a grotesque old man opened the door halfway. "Which one of ya?"

"Me!" Enoch said quickly and stepped forward.

The man opened the door all the way and a woman who could only be described as the most gorgeous woman I'd ever laid eyes on stepped out. Her dress was medieval, her hair braided down one side of her neck and hanging almost to the ground in front. Her perfect lips formed a smile as she looked at Enoch.

"Not that one." Her bright eyes turned to Eli and my blood ran cold in my aching veins. "That one."

Eli hissed under his breath and then smiled at her. "Anastasia."

"Devourer," she said, as if in awe.

"Lady," he said smoothly and bowed.

"You wish to find Magenta. And in payment for my knowledge you will lie with me?"

He nodded stiffly, but smiled.

She gasped. "Can you feel how badly I want-"

"Not yet, lady of the house," he said calmly and smiled at her in a way that was a full on blinking sign of what was to come. I felt my throat closing with anger. He turned to us. "I'll...be a while."

He turned to go and I gripped his hand tighter. He stopped and cocked his head. I didn't know if I was blowing our mission or not, but I had to say something. "What are you doing?"

"I am going with this woman and you will be quiet," he said harshly.

"Eli," I breathed and felt my heart sink. Did he know this was what would have to be done? Did he just not tell me because he knew I would refuse?

"Enoch, take Clara to get some air," he replied softer.

"Is that your mate?" Anastasia asked haughtily. I looked at her and her eyes blazed with jealousy.

"She is," Eli confirmed.

"Someone should teach her some manners," she hissed.

"Quite right." Eli glared at me openly and I shrunk back hitting Enoch's chest. "Go outside and wait for me...or I swear to you I'll dump you back in the po-dunk town I found you in!"

That was it for me. I turned so he wouldn't see the tears forming. I was utterly confused by what was happening. My only assumption was that he was either drugged, which was unlikely, or he was literally willing to do anything to save my life, regardless of what it was. Was this something I could forgive him for?

I hadn't even realized that Enoch was hauling me out into the street. He moved me to lean against the wall with my back and blocked me with his body from passing eyes. The bird had followed us out and sat near my feet.

Enoch had tried to take his place. When she emerged from the room, Enoch had said it was him seeking the information, but she refused him. I looked up at him as my fingers caressed the bracelet. Such a sweet gesture given not hours ago. "Why did you do that?"

He didn't pretend not to understand what I was asking. "Because it hurts me for you to be in pain." His face was strained and darkened. "Will you just close your eyes and rest? He'll be...done soon and we can get out of here. Stop looking at me. I can't stand it."

I wanted to make a snide comment, but it just wasn't in me. I closed my eyes and leaned my head back. That movement caused my tears to drip from my chin. Eli had been really angry with me. For him to say those things...

I sat there expecting to wait for him for ages, when he emerged in the door next to us. He pushed Enoch out of the way and grabbed my arm. He dragged me down the street, my feet tripping over the cobblestones, to another alley. He pressed me against the wall and held his hand up to Enoch. Enoch seemed to get the message as he held his hands up and turned to block the alley to anyone else.

"I didn't," Eli muttered and held my head in his hands as he pressed his forehead to mine. "I didn't, I didn't."

"What?"

"I didn't," he repeated. "I wouldn't do that. I'm so sorry, baby. Please forgive me for the way I spoke to you."

I didn't really know what to say. My insides were warring with me.

"She thinks she's a Siren." He shook his head against mine. "She trades secrets and information for…acts of service." He grimaced. "But as such, she's very easily persuaded. Her kind's minds are even more easily manipulated than humans- no offense."

"You…" I pushed him back a bit so I could see his face. "You just persuaded her to think that you…"

He nodded. "And then she told me where Magenta was. She's here, at The Wall somewhere, which is what I had hoped."

"So you didn't…"

"I didn't lay a lip or finger on her," he begged. "Believe me."

"Why couldn't you just have just said…" Crap. I knew why. There was no time. I remember the look he gave me when he realized what needed to be done. He hadn't anticipated that from her. I bit my lip.

"I said those things so you'd leave," he said, his voice harder. "Looking at your face, knowing you believed that I actually wanted to… I was about to break down and ruin our only chance of finding her. I had to get you away." He held my face again and looked at me closely. "Please forgive me."

I blew a breath and wanted to cry again. "You're forgiven, Eli. I'm sorry that I was so dense I didn't see what you were doing."

"You've been a little distracted," he said and rubbed a vein protruding from my arm. "I'm sorry."

I wrapped my arms around his neck and felt his sigh of relief as I said, "I just want to be done with this."

"Ditto that." He pressed his lips to my ear, and even in my current state of sickness and upset, I shivered as he said, "Clara, the look on your face when you thought I wanted that thing's hands on me…" He took my hand and put it on his chest. "No one is allowed to touch me every again. No matter what happens, I'll always be only yours."

I got his meaning; even if I didn't make it through this.

I got a sudden urge deep inside my gut to react to the moment. I pulled his mouth to mine and devoured him. I felt every emotion he gave me, I opened myself up to accept it and absorb it. It was like breathing your favorite perfume, eating your favorite dessert, being sung to by your favorite singer.

I fed from his love for me and his want for me. I was the one who groaned and gripped him, but he soon joined me. I felt the wall at my back as he left no space between us. I didn't know how long we stayed that way, but someone walked up behind us, their shoes clacking on the stone. I assumed it was Enoch.

Wrong assumption.

The man was tall, with a large brown Derby on his head and a cane that perfectly matched his leather shoes. He smiled. "Devourers skulking in the alleys for food. What has the world come to?"

Eli harsh breaths skated across my cheek as he looked at the stranger. Then he slowly put me behind him and pushed me with his hand on my stomach. "We aren't here to see you, Franz. We're here to see Magenta."

"But what's a little bet among friends?" He smiled wider. "Come on. My doors are always open to you."

"No thanks."

I turned to go and bumped into Enoch's chest. He had been coming to my rescue I guess. "What's up?" he asked Eli.

"Franz," he explained.

Enoch stilled and titled his head. The bird had made its way to Enoch's shoulder now. "We might can use him, you know."

"No," Eli growled.

"If we have to keep using cash, then you'll need some extra money." He grinned. "I'm game if you are. Some unsuspecting suckers are always easy game."

"Enoch, Clara is sick-"

"Yes!" he yelled and then lowered his voice. "And do you think that you can just get an easy fix from Magenta and take her back to Hillbillyville to finish up high school? No. This is far from over with the Horde. Get your head out of her butt and start thinking. We can go with Franz, win a Deuce, easy, and then we'll go to Magenta, get what we need from her and hit the road again." Eli sighed so Enoch threw out the last punch. "You know we won't outrun them without the cash. You're saving her only to kill her anyway."

"Maybe I could go to a bank in the next town and make a large withdrawal? Get out quick and hit the road," he ventured.

"Too risky and you know it. We need to get out of Dodge, a.s.a.p."

Eli looked at me, knowing full well I had no idea what they were talking about. "Pit stop," he told me. I knew whatever it was would be important so I just nodded.

"Franz," Eli called and the man immediately stepped from the shadows. Eli chuckled without humor. "Wow. I really am a sucker, huh?"

"Not a sucker," Franz offered. "A winner. A winner who plans to make a load of money tonight, along with me."

"Fine. We're in, but the girl comes with us."

"Excellent," he said and led the way. Eli walked silently with his hand wrapped around my waist. Enoch walked behind us. I kept looking up to Eli looking at his face to gauge his mood. He seemed determined, but reluctant. I was getting an emotion of regret from him which seemed weird.

"I'm fine, love," he whispered and smiled down at me. "Look, where we're going is dangerous. Franz is the leader of the rebels. They hold fights and games for betting."

"Fights?"

He nodded slowly. "Enoch and I use to come here to fight a lot. We were quite a spectacle back then." He smiled as he remembered. "We were an unbeatable match."

"Who did you fight?" I asked heard the horror in my voice.

"I said we were unbeatable," he said softly. "Don't worry. We used to fight anything that fought back. Elves, Trolls, Pixies."

"Pixies?"

He gave me a wry look. "They aren't all as sweet as they look."

"What else did you do besides fight?"

"Card games, dice, animal races. Basically anything that we could bet on, we did."

"What are you going to do now?"

"No idea. Whatever they have going on."

"Is this why you have so much money?"

"Mostly. I had to make my own after I left my parents and Enoch was all too happy helping me to beat on something for sport."

I shivered in disgust. I didn't know if I could watch him do this or not. The memory of Tate beating that guy at the match…over and over… I shook my head.

"Let's figure out what we're doing before we get distraught, ok?" he said gently.

Franz spoke then, condescending and mocking. "You are very sweet to that human girl. I wonder what you've gotten yourself into, Thames."

"I thought it was the rebel's motto to mind his own business?" Eli shot back, causing Franz to laugh.

"Indeed. No judgment here, Elijah. *That's* our motto."

Eighteen

We walked behind all the shops and I turned my eyes from the monsters prowling the corners. They left us alone and I was thankful. We arrived at the backdoor of a shack soon after we left and Franz held it open for us. The inside seemed bigger when we entered. There was a wide open space in the middle of all the bustling people looking for action.

The majority of the people present looked human, but so did Devourers so I took no stock in that notion. I knew…just knew…they were going to have to fist fight someone. The marked square in the middle, the gleam in people's eyes as they waited anxiously, the way money was changing hands at just our entrance.

Grrr…

I closed my eyes and felt his hands on my face. I peeked at him and he was smirking. He leaned forward to once again put his mouth to my ear. "I thought we agreed that you wouldn't worry. It's pouring off of you, love."

"I don't want to watch you get pounded," I said and he raised his brow in insult, "or watch you pound someone."

"Love," he started, but I put my fingers over his lips.

"Will you just go do what you have to do so we can go?"

He smiled at some private joke. Then he took me in his arms and kissed the worry right out of me. I squeaked as he leaned me back and bent me as he kissed me harder, but held me to him easily.

The sudden cheers and claps made me blush, but he kept right on kissing me. When he asked for entrance, I couldn't help but give it to him. He swept his tongue in my mouth just once before pulling me upright. His smile was full of adoration and humor. I bit my lip to stop the smile on my own face. I was mad, wasn't I?

He waited, grinning at me. I rolled my eyes and let the smile go. He grinned wider and patted my thigh as he moved to my other side, causing me to gasp. He grabbed my hand and moved me to stand next to a tall man who was standing behind a small desk looking thing with a glass room divider. "Stay here," Eli said. "I mean it, Clara Belle. You move and I'll," he shook his head and laughed, "I'll spank you harder."

"That doesn't sound like punishment," I said coyly.

He groaned and pulled me to him. He kissed the spot under my ear and said, "You *are* a temptress." He kissed me once more and then pointed at me as he made his way backwards. "Stay," he mouthed.

I nodded once and smiled. Cavuto had made his way from Enoch to me and he perched on the side of the desk. I tried to ignore him.

The man next to me held a bunch of papers in his hands and took money as people passed it over the glass. He worked frantically with the numbers in his head and on paper, his pencil flying across the pages. I looked back up just in time to see Franz take center stage. He had removed his suit jacket and the cane was gone.

A girl came up to me and nudged my shoulder with hers. "Hey."

"Hi," I said, but didn't look at her.

"I'm human. You can calm down." She giggled and I looked over at her. Or down at her I should say because she was so short. "I'm Bridgette. I'm mated, too."

"Nice to meet you, Bridgette. I'm Clara."

"Well, Clara," she said as she took my hand. "Welcome to our world."

She walked off without another word.

I turned back to Franz as he swung his arms wide and turned a slow circle in the room. "Ladies," he bowed to me, "gentleman, Devourers, Weres, Elves, Trolls, Pixies, Pikes, Daywalkers, bookies, crooks, thieves, and feelers alike. Welcome!" He bowed and then straightened looking back at Eli and Enoch, who were standing off to the side, both with their arms crossed. "We have a special treat for you. The Thames brothers!"

The applause made me feel a spike of pride for Eli, though I wasn't happy about what he was doing. I saw Eli and Enoch put their heads together as Franz went on about the rules and last chance to place bets. They smiled at each other and grasped hands as they made a decision.

It was the first time I'd ever seen them act like real brothers.

The crowd parted for the competitors and I gasped when I saw the ones they were fighting. They were huge in the torso, muscles and bulging sinew everywhere. They stood at least three feet taller than Eli and Enoch, and even had to duck when entering the arena so as not to hit their skulls on the molding.

I threw my troubled gaze to Eli, but he was already watching me. He wore a smirk and I gawked. How could he not care that he was about to get his butt handed to him?

"Last chance for bets on the Ogres!" Franz yelled and I ducked as people started barreling money and yelling over the glass.

One of the Ogres came my way and banged his fist on the glass, making me jump and yelp. It wasn't glass, it was Plexiglas. He smiled in triumphant at my reaction. But when he turned back, Eli was practically melting him with a glare.

I just crossed my arms and watched as Franz shhed the crowd. The silence was terrible and anticipatory. Then he threw his arm down and the Ogres charged. I covered my eyes with my fingers, but wound up peeking through them anyway. The Ogre swung at Enoch, but he ducked and cracked his elbow into the Ogre's spine. He was down for the count.

Eli came at the one who banged on the window and smiled tauntingly. The Ogre did the same as the other and swung for Eli's head. Eli ducked back and gave him a motion to come at him again. The Ogre roared and swung, but this time Eli kicked the Ogre's feet out from under him. I winced as the bone jarring sound of his head hitting the floor carried over the room.

The Ogre groaned, but didn't get up. That was it? That was the whole fight? The crowd erupted in curses and yells.

I looked at Eli questioningly and he shrugged as he walked towards me. He ran around the glass and took my hand before speaking to the man beside me in another language. The man laughed and clapped Eli on the back handing him a rolled-up wad of cash. He held his arm out for Cavuto and let the bird climb up his arm to his shoulder.

Eli saluted the bookie, pulled me to follow him and the people around us groaned and complained. Franz stopped us at the door. He was angry.

"Elijah, you barely let them even put up a fight! I'm not going to have much business if that's the way fights are done here. It's all about the play out!"

"Everyone knows Ogres are slower than slugs. I'm in a hurry, Franz. Maybe next time."

Eli put me in front of him and pushed our way through the back door. I began to feel another headache coming, but I didn't say anything to Eli. He was worried enough as it was. So I just said, "I thought we were in a hurry? Why the pit stop?"

"The money was too easy," Enoch explained from behind me. "And we need it to keep going."

"We?" I asked, but he didn't say anything else.

"Hey," Eli muttered and jerked his head to Enoch and then towards an old wood frame house. There was a white slash of paint above the doorframe. "A rebel camp."

"Well, we should have known there would be one if Franz is near," Enoch reasoned.

"Rebel camp?" I asked.

"A place where all of the rebels meet. They hide there and stay together."

I was intrigued. "You mean there could be other Devourers and humans who have bonded in there?" I whispered.

"Yes," Eli answered.

"Don't get any ideas," Enoch barked. "We need to keep moving."

When did he become the boss? As I was looking at him I saw a shadow move from the dark alcove. I narrowed my eyes at Finn, but Eli and Enoch had already seen him.

"Where've you been?" Enoch asked harshly.

"I've been playing, Mommy," Finn spouted. "Didn't know I had a curfew."

"It's really funny to me that you disappear the second we get here."

"Why's that funny," Finn asked. "You accusing me of something, Enoch?"

"Are you guilty of something, Finn?"

He opened his mouth to retaliate, but the door to the rebel camp opened and a young, pretty girl came out. She smiled and started to walk away, but turned. She cocked her head as she looked at me. "Clara?"

"How do you know her name?" Eli asked and pulled me closer to him.

"Bridgette told us all about you! She's waiting for you, you know," she explained calmly.

"Who?"

"You've been looking for Magenta, haven't you?"

"How do you know that?" Eli asked and again she refused to answer.

"She's in there," she said and motioned. "The attic." Eli and I looked at each other. *Attics are way creepy,* I remembered him saying.

"What are you bonded with?" Eli asked her suddenly as she tried to leave again.

She smiled and glanced at our wrist. Her smiled widened. "Ah," she said as though she understood everything now. "We don't get many Devourers who are bonded. In fact, I've only ever met one."

"Are you deliberately refusing to answer my questions?" Eli barked.

"Yes," she laughed and held up her wrist. There was a ring of…smoke around her wrist. "I'm bonded to an Elf. An Elf who hates for me to be late." She smiled as she turned to go and yelled back us. "Magenta hates to be kept waiting, too!"

"Don't, Eli," Finn said immediately. "You know they'll mark you when you go in."

"I don't care about some marking," Eli said as he stared at the door.

"You should! It's permanent!"

"Don't. Care." He looked at Enoch. "You don't have to come."

"Oh, I'm coming. I didn't come this far to turn back at the good part."

"You'll be marked," Eli threw Finn's argument at Enoch.

"So we'll match," Enoch said and marched up the stairs. "I'll even go first."

"Stop!" Finn barked and ran a hand through his hair. "This is your last chance, Eli."

"For what?" Eli said suspiciously.

"To save your soul," he growled. "We'll find another way to get rid of the bond without marking yourself for all to see as a traitor!"

"She is my soul," Eli said as he looked down at me. He tugged me gently and placed me in front of him, in between Enoch and himself. He whispered into my ear. "Don't be frightened. They are on our side, but it may take some getting used to."

Enoch knocked on the door and it opened immediately to reveal another girl. She looked at them silently. When we stayed silent as well, she cocked her brow. Eli lifted his wrist to show her the barbed string. She gasped slightly and moved aside. "Come on. Quick."

When we crossed the threshold, I felt a slice of pain in my palm. Eli and Enoch hissed, too, and we all looked down to see blood on our palms. Eli glared at her.

She sighed long and loud. "You know there's a marking to enter. The house will take its sacrifice. You are one of us now, for better or worse. Come."

We entered and I tried to ignore the stares of the people as we walked through the old house. My headache was getting worse by the second, and Eli started to notice my squint. "Love?"

"I'm ok," I answered and rubbed my forehead. There was a couple giggling near the fireplace, who stopped once they saw us. Three Devourers were watching with heated interest from the back wall, one with a girl in his lap. Another couple coming down the hall moved out of the way. The kitchen table had several people there eating what looked to be turkey sandwiches. The girl I'd spoken to at the arena, Bridgette, was there with her...Devourer! He put his arm around her protectively and watched us go cautiously.

The girl who answered the door spoke to us again. "I assume you're here to see Magenta?"

"You assume correctly," Enoch answered. "What is Magenta doing at a rebel camp?"

"There's only one reason I can think of why a bonded Devourer would need a Soothsayer," she said casually and turned to us at the bottom of the stairs. She reached out for my hand. I looked at Eli and he nodded reluctantly. She looked closely at my hand in the dimly lit house and nodded. "How long have you been sick?"

My eyes went wide. Eli jerked me behind him keeping an arm around me. "What do you know? You better start talking!"

"I know nothing, but I have eyes and she looks terrible, no offense. And your blood on your hand…"

I lifted my hand to look at it. My palm was stained with streaks of red and steaks of blue. I jerked my hand behind me. I leaned my head against Eli's back. I felt my blood rushing and pounding behind my eyes. I was getting worse and there was nothing to stop it. Eli turned and scooped me up in his arms.

"Take us to Magenta," he ordered.

She nodded once and lifted her arm to the stairs as she moved aside. Eli made quick work of the steps and went to the only door that there was. Enoch opened it and it led to another set of stairs. He took them two at a time. Eli followed at a steadier pace for my benefit. He kissed my hair and said it would be ok.

"Magenta?" Enoch called out. "We need a word, madam."

"That you do," a grave and crackled voice called out. Eli set my feet down gently, but held me to him.

"Madam," he said gently. "We come offering anything you wish, if you'll tell us what we need to do. My bond mate is sick."

"The kind of sick that can't be fixed just-like-that, I'm afraid," she answered. She was sitting on a couch, the middle sunken in and dingy. Her dress was old fashioned and the blue faded. She was old and her fingers were crippled by arthritis. I wasn't sure how, but I could tell she'd once been very beautiful.

She gestured for us to sit across from her and turned the lamp on next to her with a wave of her fingers. I tried not to gawk as we settled on the opposite couch. Cavuto perched himself on the lamp top, basking in the fake UV rays.

The walls were lined with old desks and bookcases, with bottles of herbs and...things.

"Now," she started and smiled a toothless smile. "You bonded him to you, did ya now, girl?"

"Yes, ma'am...uh, madam."

She laughed and then turned serious. "That's strike one."

Eli leaned forward. "What do you mean?"

"I get to ask the questions, not you," she muttered and turned back to me. Her gaze roamed me and she settled on my eyes. "One bonded green, one Devourer purple." She tsked. "Quite a pickle you got yo'selves in."

I nodded as she continued to stare at me.

"And just what is it you think I can do for you?"

Eli answered. "We want a cure."

"Or the bond to be removed," Enoch supplied. "Whatever releases her from the sickness."

She laughed. "Now you know I can't be removing no bonds. You know better 'an that."

"There has to be something-"

"There's nothing," she barked and glared at him. "And if you came here just to free yo'self from the bond, you wasted a perfectly good Witch's stone to get here."

"No, madam," Eli placated. "We came just to see what could be done for Clara. She's been sick ever since…"

"Ever since she took your blood," Magenta supplied and smirked, her wrinkled face lifting.

Nineteen

"How would you know that?" Eli asked as I got up. I could no longer sit there on that couch so still. I walked to the bookcase and found a picture of her. The dress looked the same to me. I eyed her.

"She's got poisoned blood. Your blood, however she got it in her, is fighting her human blood to rule."

"We know all that," Eli said and growled in frustration. "We determined all that already. I want to know how to fix it."

"Can't be fixed." She smiled. "But have a nice trip back."

"You were very pretty, if I can say that," I told her as I examined the photo. Right next to it was a little clear box labeled 'Goblin's Teeth', but the teeth were huge and long. I felt myself frown.

"You may say it," she spouted, "but flattery will get you nowhere. Strike two." I felt my eyes widen in surprise. She apparently didn't like compliments. I went back to my seat beside Eli as he went on talking to her.

"Madam, I know you know something," he accused.

"You don't deserve a cure!" she accused back.

"Why do you say that?"

"Tell her," she said and looked at me. "Tell her the real reason you want to save her."

The breath stilled in my lungs. What did she mean? I looked at Eli. He seemed at a loss as he said, "I love her."

"That's not good enough."

"I love her!" he roared. "She bound herself to me and I want to save her."

"Tell her the truth!" she said just as loudly and waited.

He gulped and looked at me again. His eyes held something… It made me feel funny as I waited for something he obviously had to say. And then his guilt hit me and I held my sob back. Oh, no…

"I want to save her because…" Even though he was speaking to her, he never took his eyes off mine. "Because I'm a better man with her. Because I can't imagine going back to being who I was before I met her. Because I'm afraid…that I could be that monster again without her here loving me." He touched my cheek with the backs of his fingers. "I'm sorry, love, for being so selfish."

Selfish? I turned my glare to Magenta. She seemed amused, which put some fuel into my pissed-off meter. "How dare you?"

Eli took a swift breath in surprise of my comment. Magenta just kept smiling. "Clara," he chastised.

"How dare you judge the whys of our relationship," I kept going. "You want me to be angry at him for feeling that way? Well I don't. Isn't that what love is supposed to be? Completely consumed by someone to the point that even the thought of not being with them through eternity is agony? He loves me, I don't doubt that. And I love him. If I had to go back to my life before him...I can't imagine that hell."

"Is that really how you feel?" she asked after a pause.

"Yes."

"Strike three. I'm afraid I can't do a whole lot for you," she said and leaned forward. "Love is beautiful, keen, tenacious, willing, all consuming an' sacrificial. I see all of dat in ya both. But the problem is that the sacrifice of love sometimes costs us more than we pay."

"But..." I thought hard of a way to convince her. "If it's love you're looking for-"

"It's not." She leaned back and looked contemplative. "You got three strikes which means you're deserving. You sure are deserving of it, girl. But I'm sorry. *You've* sacrificed all there is. *You* have nothing left to give."

My throat caught on a sob. "So this is it for me?"

"You won't survive if the Devourer blood wins. I'm sorry."

"No," Eli voiced a tortured plea. "No, please, madam."

"It's out of my hands," she told us and looked at Eli long and hard. He eventually turned away from her and gripped me behind my neck to pull me to him. He shhed me as another sob broke through. His face was a picture of agony as he tried to soothe me.

Enoch cursed and stood. "That can't be the end of it."

She spoke in that same haunting tone, "There is nothing *you* can do either."

"Well..." He looked at Eli and I knew what was coming. I begged him silently not to say it, but he was an idiot. "The bond will break this way. At least she can go peacefully and you can be you again."

Eli put me aside gently and lunged for him. I put my head in my hands and refused to watch and Eli shoved Enoch to the wall. He growled all sorts of things in his brother's face before backing up. His eyes were wild as he looked at me and came to help me stand. "Come on, love. Let's go home."

I didn't want to, but I let him take me. The thought of Mrs. Ruth and Pastor trying to figure out what was wrong with me and watching me die was not an option.

I thought about that as Eli led me silently down the stairs. Bridgette was standing at the bottom of them, waiting with her mate and a whole group of others silently. It was as if they'd been expecting us to leave unhappy. She patted my arm as we passed.

Enoch followed behind, but was silent as well. My mind raced. We arrived back at The Wall entrance and Eli found the sliver. We went through, but he let it go just in time to stop Enoch. I heard him muttering as he opened it for himself.

We walked through the brush and moved the large branches from our way, and then we were on the bank again. It wasn't until we were there that I realized we left Cavuto.

"Cavuto," I said to Eli.

"He's fine where he is. It's better for him there anyway."

Then bright lights were suddenly shone on us from the trees. It hurt so bad that I screamed as I pressed my face into Eli's shirt front. My senses were still on high alert. It was dark here now, but we had company.

"Well, well, well," someone said and laughed. "Thames boys."

"So tacky to start off a villainous speech with *well, well, well,*" Enoch snorted, but when I glanced at him he looked peeved. "Didn't Hatch teach you that before we put him in Resting Place?"

"Are you admitting to being a traitor along with your brother?" the man asked. He moved forward to block a stream of the headlights. I could see a little better. They were about five or six cars out there.

The Horde.

"Traitor is a strong word," Enoch muttered.

"Boys," the man said. "Let's not keep them waiting."

"Where, Reece?" someone else yelled and he looked around.

"Doesn't matter. Retribution can happen anywhere."

Retribution! That's what Finn said the Horde wanted to do to Eli. I cringed into his side as I heard so many people moving around us. Eli kissed my forehead, his eyes shut tightly. Before I even realized what was happening, I heard scuffles and something was thrown over Eli's head. Then mine.

This time when my head seemed to explode, it wasn't my headache to blame, it was someone's fist.

~ ~ ~

I woke with a gasp. My head was still covered and I heard them talking around me. My earplugs had been removed. Eli was begging them not to do something. I'd never heard him so desperate before. I tried to move, but arms were holding mine. Then I felt the chill of the wind and flushed as I realized they'd taken my shirt off. I was bare except for my bra from the waist up.

I wiggled, but the arms clamped on me tighter. The bag was snatched from my head to reveal Eli in a similar situation. His shirt was off and he was being held by three Devourers across from me in a small clearing of the bushes. He shook his head over and over as if trying to remove a thought.

Enoch was off to the side, his neck twisted at a sick angle. He'd be pissed when he woke up later.

"I'm Reece," the man from before said. "I'm the new leader of the Horde, thanks to you and your tame Devourer."

I said nothing. My gaze flickered from Reece's to Eli's. They had built a fire in between us and when he reached for something I knew what they were going to do. I begged with everything that was in me.

"Please don't. Please. Take me and destroy me, do whatever you want." I was dying anyway right? "But please don't burn Eli again."

They all laughed reluctantly, as if they couldn't believe what I was saying. Reece spoke, his voice full of malicious joy. He twisted the brand iron in his fingers. "Sweetheart," he crooned sweetly. "This isn't for Eli. This is for you."

My heart stopped. Well…at least if they didn't do Eli again… I looked at Eli and tried to push as much resolve into my stare as possible. Then Finn came forward from the back masses. My heart stopped for the second time.

"Finn?" Eli accused.

"I warned you," he said. "I told you not to go into the rebel camp. That was it. That was when I knew there was no saving you." He crossed his arms. "You fed Angelina to the Horde to save yourself."

"She's the one who called them, not me."

"You fed her to them to save yourself!" he repeated in a yell.

Eli stopped and twisted his lips. "Yes. I did that. I let them take her knowing full well that I was lying to them."

Finn looked like he'd been punched. Then he nodded. "You knew I was obsessed with her."

"You knew she *wasn't* obsessed with you."

"But I bet she will be now," he said and smiled suddenly. My eyes grew to impossible size as a healthy and happy Angelina emerged. He opened his arm for her and she went right to it. "Now that I've brought down the ultimate traitor in our race and handed the Horde an unsuspecting rebel camp." He laughed at our expressions. "A little History lesson? Angelina joined the Horde when she realized you were a lost cause. They followed you and kept tabs on you. When she told them about Clara, they knew it was only a matter of time before you sought out a rebel camp. We'd never have guessed they'd plant one smack in the middle of The Wall!" He laughed. "That was a pleasant surprise. You all made it just a little too easy. Now, we're going to make an example of you."

Angelina smiled at me, but said nothing. I wondered about the train. Could that nightmare have been a reverie?

Eli's head hung in defeat. I tried to send him my love, I tried to force some calm and resolve toward him. His eyes jerked up.

He shook his head again, his face lined with blue angry veins. "Stop it, Clara! Stop it! Reece," he implored, "listen to me. I'll give you everything I have. I have two accounts, each with at least a couple hundred grand. Take them. Take anything you want. Burn me, burn me for the rest of my life! Please, man, just please don't do this to her."

"Such sweet sorrow from you, Eli," Reece mocked, "but I'm afraid we have no deal."

He let the stick dance in the flames for a moment and then moved forward to me. I heard Eli's grunts and pleas from behind Reece, but I was too focused on the glowing end of the stick he was about to press into my skin.

Then he switched directions mid-stride and went straight to Eli.

"On second thought," he muttered and looked back at me as he pressed it to Eli's chest right on the spot he already had a scar. I screamed as Eli held it in, his face and arms blue with the strain and anger. Then Reece stopped.

He put it back in the fire…and came my way. My breaths were so fast I felt lightheaded. I steeled myself, hearing Eli's yells and pleas behind Reece. And then the most blinding pain I'd ever had seared through my chest as he pressed the circle brand over my heart. I turned my head and didn't know if I was screaming or not. My senses were still high and everything seemed to echo around me. He kept pressing me, the seconds turning into minutes.

Then Reece was hit from the side and thrown into the fire. He yelled and rolled to get out. Enoch stood, his angry blue veins standing at attention as he blurred to stand in front of me. Reece stood, his clothes burned in spots, but otherwise fine.

"You can't fight us all, Enoch."

"Good thing he won't have to," a voice called from the woods and suddenly we were being swarmed. The rebel camp. They were risking exposure, risking their lives for us. Why?

The men who held me released me and I fell against my will to the ground. Eli was there in seconds as the melee went on around us. He didn't care about anything but me. He didn't say anything, just picked up my upper half and held me to him, careful of my burn. I pushed him back a little and saw the angry mark on his chest was already starting to heal. I let my fingers hover over it as he watched me.

"I'm so sorry-" he began, but it was a pointless effort.

"You could no sooner hurt me than I could hurt you. Stop it." I started to shake, my arms and fingers twitching.

"You're going into shock," he told me and held me gently.

"No," I said and felt it. Deep down, I knew. "It's getting worse. Eli, I'm -"

"Don't you dare say those words," he growled and pressed his head to mine. "Just stay with me."

"I love you."

He cursed softly. "I love you," he said through gritted teeth. "I love you, Clara, and I'll always be only yours."

I felt the tears come. The ache in my chest was unbearable for two reasons: the burn and the heartache. I reached up to kiss him and he met me half way. His lips were wet and I opened my eyes to see his face streaked with tears. My breath caught as I reached for his cheek. He didn't shy away, ashamed, he just watched me as I examined the wetness. Real tears. Not blue or supernatural. Just real, salty tears.

I kissed him again, and we soon realized that the noise had died down. I peeked my eyes open to find an army. There had to be at least a hundred of them. The Horde was down on the ground. Of course they weren't dead, but they were down for now.

Bridgette pulled a bag off of her shoulder and knelt down beside us. "Let me put something on this," she said and rummaged through her bag. She brought out a small cloth and a bandage. She opened the cloth, folding down the corners to reveal some small leaves. She poured a little water on the leaves from her water bottle and they sizzled. She smiled as I shied away. "It's ok."

She put the wet leaves on my skin gently with her thumb and secured the bandage. Eli found my shirt on the ground near us and pulled it over my head. Then he pulled me into his lap. The masses had gathered around the fire and we all soaked in the moment. Finally Franz came forward, giving Eli a wry smile. "I tried to get you stay at The Wall if you recall."

"How did you do all this? How did you know that we needed you?"

He sat down and the others followed suit. "The Horde has been hovering around. Asking questions. Going to the clubs. We knew they were up to something. And then you show up…bonded to a human." He smiled. "We knew that was the reason."

"But why help us?" Eli's brow bunched. "We brought them to your front door basically."

"Because that's what rebels do. Because we'd like you to join us. Because most of us know what it's like to be in your shoes. Because sometimes the sacrifice of love costs too much to pay by yourself."

Twenty

"We should go," Eli said. "They'll wake up soon."

"Nah," Franz said and laughed. "Those boys and girls are down for the count."

"What do you mean?"

He nodded to someone and he dragged a body in the middle of us. The Devourer had a large…tooth protruding from his chest. I peeked up. His eyes were black. Goblins?

"How? How did you…" Eli asked.

"Goblin's teeth," Franz explained. "A Goblin's bite is what paralyzes them, that doesn't mean the Goblin has to do the actual biting." He grinned.

"Goblin's teeth," Eli said as if tasting the phrase.

"Cavuto," I explained. "Cavuto kept saying 'A Goblin's tooth is all you need'. But how did he know? And why are the teeth so big when they look so small on a Goblin?"

"Big gums," someone said and they all laughed.

"Well," Eli said and sighed. "I really appreciate what you did, but I need to get Clara home." He looked and me and swallowed. "She needs to see her family…"

"We won't keep you, but we'd love it if you'd stay. Or visit. There aren't that many of us rebels anymore," Franz said sadly.

Eli nodded and helped me stand. I looked up at him. Something was gnawing at me. Something wanting to make itself known. It felt like we had unfinished business. Maybe that was just my subconscious not wanting to admit that it was almost over.

"Well, like I said before," Franz said and paused. "Nothing wrong with asking for help every now and again. The sacrifice of love is sometimes more than you can pay."

"Why does everyone keep saying that?" Enoch said in a huff.

"It's something Magenta says," Franz explained and turned back to Eli. "She's been with us for a few years now. I know you were wondering."

But Eli was lost in thought. He cocked his head slowly as if catching some idea. Then he gasped and looked at me. Everyone waited patiently for him to work it out, and his face split with the biggest grin. He grabbed my face gently and kissed me. "That old bat and her riddles," he mused.

"What?"

"She said you couldn't pay the sacrifice!" he explained and grinned. "She didn't say I couldn't."

"What are you-"

"No time." He cursed. "Ah! We don't have a Witch's stone to get back in."

"You mean one of these?" Franz said and held a stone between his fingers. "We have a few young Witches who aspire to be rebels," he said and grinned as a girl came forward. She wrapped her arms around his waist and shook her head good naturedly. She was the Witch, I assumed. His Witch. She wasn't old and crusty like the others I'd seen though.

"Franz, thank you," Eli said sincerely.

"No sweat. Let's go."

~ ~ ~

We ran down the streets of the market all the way back to the rebel camp house. Enoch grumbled all the way behind us. Eli burst through the doors and took me all the way back upstairs. Magenta was in the same spot she'd been in when we left. She smiled when we entered…and even looked a little relieved.

"You returned." Then her smile slipped. "And not a moment too soon."

She was looking at me. Eli turned and did a double take. He lifted his hand and rubbed the end of my nose. He brought it back and there was blue on his thumb. I was bleeding…Devourer blood. Oh, no.

He rushed on. "I get it. I'm here to offer the sacrifice. The sacrifice that Clara couldn't pay, I'm here to pay it. Tell me what to do."

"It's a little mo' complicated than all that, Eli." She motioned for us to sit again. Enoch was there again. For a guy who hated me, he sure was stuck to me like glue. "The sacrifice that is required may be more than you can pay as well."

Eli slumped in anger once more. "What do you mean? No more riddles, Magenta, just tell me!"

"I didn't tell you before because you had to figure it out for yo'self. But now that you have, I'll tell you this." She leaned forward. "The sacrifice you haft to make is you."

"What?" I said angrily. "No."

"My life for hers?" Eli said calmly.

"Your essence," she said cryptically. "See…the way to fix her is to stab her." Eli gasped and stood up to yell, she held up her hand. "Stab her to kill the Devourer blood with a Goblin's tooth. The Devourer in her will die…but so will the Devourer in you. Through da bond."

"Eli!" Enoch boomed. "You can not do this!"

I felt all the breath leave me.

Oh, no. I just lost him, didn't I? I couldn't ask him to do that. To be human for me? It was too much. And judging by Eli's cool calm it was too much for him, too. This was it. The sacrifice of love was sometimes too much to pay, as she had said. There was no way Eli would-

He pulled my face up from its dejected downward gaze. "I would sacrifice anything and everything." He shook his head. "This isn't really even a sacrifice." He looked at her. "I've wanted nothing but to be human since the day I met her."

I pulled his face back to look at mine with a jerk. He had? Was that true? But why? Humans were weak and required sleep and couldn't do reveries with each other.

"The only other option," she ventured, "is to have her in a perpetual state of reverie."

"That's not a life, that's a prison for her."

"What's she talking about?" I asked.

He rubbed the bond on my wrist with his thumb. "She's saying that I can take your body somewhere and bring you into a reverie…but never let you out of it." He swallowed. "Your body would be frozen in time, no aging, no getting sicker. We'd live in the reverie forever, doing whatever we wanted, going wherever we wanted to go."

"Is that what you want?"

"I don't think it's a life. You'd never see your family. You'd only ever see me for the rest of eternity and we'd be stuck in a dream world forever."

"That doesn't sound so bad," I said quietly.

"It doesn't sound so *good*, either," Eli rebutted.

"But the other option…you don't want to be human. You're just saying that because I am."

The corner of his mouth turned up as he spoke. "To be someone who no longer fights an evil nature, to be someone who can eat and sleep with you, have real live dreams of you, marry you, have kids with you and a white fence and live only one lifetime?" He smiled. "That doesn't sound like a sacrifice, that sounds like paradise."

"Really?" I squeaked.

"Really." He kissed me. "I never wanted you to be what I am, but I would give anything to be what you are."

I fought not to break down. I never thought I'd be loved this way by anyone. He was going to give up everything for me...

He stroked my cheek with his fingers before looking back to Magenta. "But once again, it's not really a sacrifice. It's what I've wanted, so I don't get how this counts."

"You becoming human isn't the sacrifice," she said plainly. "What's da most awful thing you can think of when it comes to her?"

His eyes moved back and forth as he thought. Then his eyes widened and he looked at her, his face etched in horror. "I have to do it. I have to stab her."

"Yes." She smiled grimly. "The sacrifice for you...is living your worst nightmare."

He jumped up and prowled the room with heavy boot falls. He ran his hands through his hair and then stopped. He looked at Magenta seriously. "Will she feel the pain? Will the Devourer just fade away, or will it fight?"

She just looked back at him and that was answer enough. He groaned and went back to prowling. Enoch stood and sighed. "Why does everything have to be so complicated? I'll stab her."

Any other time, I could have seen the irony and humor of this whole thing, but I knew what Magenta's answer would be.

"It has to be the one who would despise the act most." She gave him a wry look. "And everyone here knows that is most definitely not you. It's the whole point of a sacrifice."

"Clara," Eli said ignoring them. "I don't know if..."

"Come. Sit by me." He came over and I thought he'd sulk next to me, but he gripped my hand, his fingers playing with mine. He rubbed my promise ring with care. I looked back to Magenta. "Tell me what it'll be like?" I asked, but my voice was breathy from the headache I was having.

She sighed and out of nowhere Cavuto came and perched on the side of the couch. She began, "The blood will fight. It won't just be paralyzed like when a Devourer dies. It'll be torture as the blood drains from you. Then when you wake up, your human body will have to be tended to for its wounds from the stab."

"So he stabs me with the Goblin's tooth…then my body rids itself of the bad blood…and then I'm normal again?"

"If your human wounds can be tended to quickly enough, then yes."

I swung my gaze to Eli, who watched me warily. "Eli, can you do this?"

"I want to be human, I do, and I want to help you. I just can't see myself sticking that thing into your chest," he whispered and looked at me with pain in his eyes. "The reason I almost left before was because I was afraid of hurting you. And now to have to literally hurt you… It's my worst fear. It's my kryptonite. Clara…"

I scrunched my brow and tried to think, but the pounding behind my eyes was persistent. Could I stab Eli if the situation were reversed? I wanted to think that I would. I understood though, it sucked. I also understood that Eli would do it in the end, but he needed to put up a fight with himself about it. So I let him. He and Magenta went back and forth about other options and the lack of.

I didn't listen. The bird squawked about the Goblin's tooth, but I drowned him out with my own thinking. Enoch sat in silence on my other side. I glanced at him. He glanced at me. We stared at each other. We didn't know if

I would live or not. But if I did live through this, he knew Eli would be human and he'd be forced to hate him.

I was taking his brother away from him and didn't shy away from the look of scorn that I so deserved. Did Eli understand? Did he know fully that he was choosing me over his brother?

I went to ask him, but screamed instead as a pain shot through my spine and skull so hard that I fell back onto the couch. I clawed at my chest as it ripped open. Surely there was blood everywhere. I lifted my shirt to find the bandage from the burn and nothing else. Eli was frantic to find out what was wrong, but I could hear nothing. Not a sound…

I reached up to my ear and when it came back it was covered in blue blood. Eli gripped my hand and examined the blood. Enoch was yelling at him and he yelled back. I lay there and waited to be claimed by darkness, but for good this time. We waited too late…it was too late.

The last thing I saw as I lay on the couch with Eli hovering over me was him reaching his hand out and Magenta giving him what he asked for. Then he raised his arms above him, his mouth open in silent cry, and he plunged it into my chest.

Twenty One

I was in hell.

I was being lifted and could do nothing to stop whoever it was, though my skin was practically boiling from my bones. I begged them to stop, but they couldn't hear me or wouldn't listen.

The jostling was the most painful thing I'd ever experienced. I felt raw and open and on fire. And then everything went black once more.

~ ~ ~

My eyes opened to night sky above me. I felt like I was drowning. I still couldn't hear. I wiped my face. There was a wetness all over me and in my nose. I gasped to breath and lifted my hands to see them covered in blood; blue and red.

Eli pulled my body a little to look at him. He was running through the trees with me in his arms. He was saying something, but I couldn't hear the words. I read his lips for some it. He mouthed, "Hold on, love. Hold on."

My head leaned back, lolling and giving up its quest to hold itself up. I let go and the darkness took me prisoner. And I welcomed it.

~ ~ ~

All around me was red and blue. It flashed and I woke with a startle. We were in an ambulance. No…we were running passed one. Then the lights were so bright as Eli rushed us through double doors, I threw my arm over my eyes and felt it in my chest when I groaned.

Then the tug of war started.

Eli was fighting with someone over me. I opened my eyes to see Eli refusing to relinquish his hold on me so they could take me in the back.

We were at a hospital. Ah. They were trying to take me to a room and they didn't want him in there with me. I rolled my head to the side to see a sign on the wall, but it was in Spanish. We must still be in Arequipa, or near it. My body had a sudden convulsion that had me seizing. Eli laid me on the table and stepped back as they took over, ripping off my shirt and starting IVs. I saw him mouth, "Oh, God, please," while he gripped his head and closed his eyes tightly.

When I looked back at them, the lights were so bright that everyone had halos around their heads. But I knew they weren't halos because I wasn't in heaven. These were not angels.

I was still in hell.

~ ~ ~

The smell of flowers filled my senses. I felt my lips part, cracked and thirsty, as I took a breath. My eyes wouldn't open. It felt like they were stuck...or something. I tried to say something, but my throat was too dry and it came out a wheeze.

A straw was placed between my lips and I drawled greedily at it, moaning at the coolness and comfort it offered me. When it was taken away, I lifted my hand to touch my eyes. Tape. My eyes were taped shut.

"Let me, love," Eli said gently and took my hand laying it back to the bed. He peeled the tape off and it hurt, but nothing had ever hurt as much as my chest did when I took a deep breath. I palmed my wound and felt the thick bandages under my fingers. Eli took my hand once more and moved it back to the bed. "Don't," he said softly.

When my eyes were freed, I opened them. Eli was there in the chair right up against my bed. His eyes had dark circles under them and his skin was pale with worry. He lifted his hand to rub my cheek and I sighed. Then he sighed at my reaction and laid his head to my hand, kissing it over and over.

"Another hospital, huh?" I asked.

"Had to," he replied and lifted his head. His eyes were pained.

"What are all the flowers for?"

He sighed. "The story Enoch apparently told them was that we were attacked and robbed. They don't take kindly to their tourists being treated that way I guess. The flowers and cards have been pouring in. They talked about you on the news a little bit, too. About how the police are looking non-stop. I feel kind of bad about that."

"Huh. Well, at least they believed it." I touched my eyes again. "So I'm back to normal? My eyes are back to green and my blood is good old red?"

He nodded and gulped as he let his eyes roam my face. "I am…so sorry."

"No, I'm sorry." His brow bunched. "I didn't get a chance to ask you about Enoch. About choosing me over him. Wait…where is he?"

"He's gone," Eli said casually. "He left as soon as the…bond broke."

I started to sit up, but the lancing pain was enough of a reminder that that wasn't a good idea. I groaned, but tried to keep it to a minimum. I knew who'd be feeling a double dose of guilt over this one. He pressed my shoulders down and grimaced. I said, "What do you mean the bond broke?"

"The Devourer blood is gone. He left as soon as the string left his wrist." His breath stuttered and one tear slid down his face. "You…died, Clara. For one minute, you were dead." His face twisted and he wiped his eyes with his thumb and forefinger. "I thought I killed you."

"So because I died, the bond broke?" I lifted my arm to see my own wrist. The bond was still there, connecting me to Eli. I looked at him in confusion. He cracked his first smile that made my heart leap and bound.

"You and I are still bound," he said and his voice almost growled in that happy way when he was thoroughly pleased. "But Enoch is free."

I thought about what he was saying. Why would the bond release Enoch? The bond was a connection from one human to one Devourer…I gasped. Eli wasn't a Devourer anymore…was he? I took in his appearance. He looked terrible. He hadn't slept, that I could tell, and his lips were dry and cracked like mine, like he hadn't drunk anything. He looked so tired…

"Eli, you're... You... I'm so sorry!" I said and reached out my arm. "How long have I been out?"

"Only a day," he comforted and kissed my palm. "But why are you sorry?"

"You've been human for a whole day? And all alone, no one was here to help you?"

"You were here." His thumb rubbed under my eye, wiping away my errant tear. "You were all I needed."

"But-"

"But nothing." He smiled. "It happened here, at the hospital. The blood was coming out of you, but by the time we got here, most of the Devourer blood was gone. And when the last drop left you, I felt it."

"Felt what?" I said enraptured.

"Hunger." He laughed. "I was hungry. As the day wore on, I felt tired and sleepy and then exhausted, too. It was wonderful."

"Did you sleep?"

"Not a wink. I couldn't stop looking at you."

"Did you eat?" I asked.

He laughed. "No. I didn't want the growling in my stomach to stop. I wanted to feel it; to know I was human and it wasn't a dream. I wanted to wait for you to wake up."

"Well, I'm awake." I smiled, though my face hurt to do it. "Are you still hungry?"

"Famished." His grin was beautiful.

"Eli..." The tears came once more. "You risked everything for me."

"You *gave* everything to me," he groaned happily and kissed my forehead. "You saved me again, Clara Belle."

"You saved me."

He scoffed, but smiled sadly. "By stabbing you?"

"By doing what needed to be done." I groaned. "Ah, they called Pastor didn't they?"

"Uh…no." He looked guilty. "I lied. I told them we were married and here on our honeymoon."

I smiled. "You did? You persuaded them?"

"I can't do that anymore, love."

Oh, yeah. "Right."

"I just used my natural charm." He kissed my forehead again and stayed close. "It works on the ladies apparently."

"Hey," I complained softly.

He laughed soundlessly, his lips curving in a smile against my skin. And then he did something that had me smiling as the tears made their way down to my lips.

He sang me back to sleep.

Honey, you should know,

that I could never go on without you.

Green eyes

Honey, you are the sea

upon which I flow.

And I came here to talk

I think you should know.

Green eyes

you're the one that I wanted to find.

And anyone who tried to deny you,

must be out of their minds.

Because I came here with a load

and it feels so much lighter since I met you.

Honey, you should know

that I could never go on without you.

Green Eyes.

Twenty Two

We spent the next few days doing just that. We watched bad Spanish soap operas because that was all that was on. We talked about everything that had happened and nothing of what was to come. We drank. We ate. The first thing I did the day that I woke up in the hospital was get Eli to order us both a tray of food. I barely touched mine, I just wanted him to eat. And he did. I made a joke about how he had to start watching himself or he'd get a burger gut now that calories counted.

The train ride home five days later was torture. The hospital tried to get me to stay longer, but I refused. I had slept most of the time anyway and poor Eli just stayed in my room in that horrible chair. Eli had been speaking to Mrs. Ruth. He wanted to wait for my go ahead, and once he had it he called them. The hospital was a bare minimum kind of place and didn't have phones in the rooms. Or bathrooms, or windows. So, I couldn't speak to her myself as I was confined to my bed. I was glad to go to say the least.

But Mrs. Ruth had apparently run Eli up the river. He could no longer persuade her that everything was fine and they wanted to drop everything and come and get me. I told him to please beg her not to come. He managed somehow to convince her that by the time they got their emergency passports and got here, it would be time to go home again.

She wasn't happy. We were in another country for crying out loud. I wondered how long I'd be grounded for this.

And now, on the train ride home I was anxious. I thought about what my mom would have done with this situation. She would have been worried, but she would have also made a comment about how this stunt would ruin my reputation. I would have rolled my eyes and she would've said she was serious. That my reputation as a lady hinged my future.

I shook my head. She had been a small town thinker through and through, but I'd gladly listen to a lecture about my reputation right now just to hear her voice.

"Hey," he said, pulling me from my thoughts. I looked his way and smiled as he munched on a bag of Doritos. "You ok? The train's jostling isn't too much, is it?"

I shook my head. "I'm good," I told him and leaned my head on his shoulder and wrapped my arm around his. "Just thinking."

"Mrs. Ruth and the Pastor will be waiting for you at the station," he said carefully.

"Waiting for us," I corrected. "I may be grounded for the rest of my life, but they are going to just have to accept you. You're mine now, Mr. Thames."

He grinned and leaned his head to mine. "I sure am. And you're mine, Mrs…" He opened his eyes and sat up. His face took on a brightness that could only be described as joy. He slid down to his knees on the floor before me. My smiled slipped. What was he doing? He pushed my knees apart to kneel between them and took my face in his hands. "CB. It's crazy. It's stupid. The Pastor will probably never allow it. You're too young and I'm too old. It's…" He chuckled, his happy breath on my face. "It's everything that I want and everything I don't deserve." I waited, my lips parted. My eyes flicked to the others near us on the train and saw they were watching us. We all waited for Eli to finish, to say that one thing. "Clara, will you be my Mrs. Thames?"

Wow. He was right. It was stupid. It was crazy. We hadn't even graduated yet. And the Pastor was going to murder him for sure... I couldn't stop my grin as I nodded. My tongue refused to say the words, but he seemed satisfied with my answer. He pulled me to him and kissed me gently.

The claps resounded around us and I felt my blush under his hands, but I still found myself pulling his shirt front in my fingers and dragging him to me. Then I winced at my stupidity as the stitches in my chest pulled. I laughed as he fussed over me and I kissed him again. He tucked me into his body and I fit perfectly there.

We fit *together* perfectly.

~ ~ ~

"Here we go," Eli said in my ear and let me loose from his arm so Mrs. Ruth could hug me.

I warded her off with my hands in an effort to slow her advance. She gripped my arms first and slowly brought me in for a hug. Pastor stared at Eli with barely contained anger. Eli offered his hand to him, and a sincere apology with a promise to explain everything later. Well, not everything.

Pastor sighed and shook his hand. Mrs. Ruth hadn't released me yet and I patted her back to get her to. She leaned back. "Are you ok?"

I nodded. "I am. I know you're mad-"

"Mad?" She shook her head. "Clara…you're practically a woman. You're graduating, you've made your choices for your future and there's nothing we can do to stop that. We just want you to know that we're here for you. I don't know what you have planned, but we have no intentions of tossing you to the world as soon as you graduate. You're always welcome with us…and we love you, honey."

Well didn't that just make the guilt taste sweeter. "I know you don't understand." I bit my lip. "But I…" I looked at Eli. "Eli's… We had a few things we needed to do. Important things that changed everything for me. Eli saved my life."

"What?" Pastor barked and came to stand in front of us. "What did you say?"

"Eli saved me in Arequipa. More than once."

"But the news said you were mugged and taken to the hospital."

"They didn't have all of the facts. Eli carried me- carried me in his arms all the way to the hospital and never left my side for a second."

I looked back at Eli and almost laughed at how human he looked. He was blushing and it made him so irresistibly cute. He looked around uncomfortably and when Mrs. Ruth launched herself at him, I thought he'd bolt. But he hugged her back and let her faun on him with her 'Oh, thank you's. But then she leaned back and said sternly, "However, you're not off the hook for taking her there in the first place."

He nodded. "Yes ma'am."

Pastor wrapped an arm around my shoulder and kissed my forehead. "So this is what I have to look forward to when all my other kids are teenagers?" he joked.

My other kids…he called me his kid.

I hugged him hard, taking him by surprise. He seemed to understand it was what I needed. He hugged and rocked me gently, letting me bask in the first moment of calm in a long while.

~ ~ ~

"Oh. My. Gosh!" Ariel cried when I called. "I can't believe that! Did they find the guy who did it? Were you really hurt? Where was Eli? How did I not see this on the news!"

I told her what I could and lied about the rest. She told me about her and Patrick. They were a thing now and she was as giddy as I'd ever heard her. I couldn't wait to get back to school - and it sickened me to say that - but it was true. Mrs. Ruth said I could go back at the end of the week.

And Eli.

Well, Eli was allowed at the house on weeknights like a normal boyfriend. And at night when I closed my eyes, I was all by myself in my dreams. He was a normal, human guy. He still lived at his house, but intended to sell it once we graduated and decided what we wanted to do.

We hadn't told anyone about Eli asking me to marry him. Everyone would just throw a fit because there was no way they could understand. We were far from a normal couple, and we intended to wait a while. Mrs. Ruth would love to plan a wedding, I was sure, and I intended to give her the opportunity. But I didn't want to wait too long…

~ ~ ~

Eli came to walk me to school that Friday, my first day back in almost two weeks. I had a lot of catching up to do. He waited outside for me and smiled that smile when he saw me. He kissed my forehead and took my hand.

That was it and that was what had been happening all week. He was ever so gentle and careful of me, but I was ready to start being normal again. I felt pretty good. And I was having some serious Eli lip withdrawals.

Ariel and Patrick met us in the school quad. Patrick was not shy about letting it be known to everyone that they were together. I smiled at Ariel and shook my head. All that worry for nothing.

Everyone wanted to know where Eli and I had been. The rumor that won out among most students was that I had gotten pregnant and we'd run away to get married. I rolled my eyes at their lame gossip.

Prom was coming up and graduation. Only a couple more weeks and we'd be free. I wasn't worried about life after high school. I was looking forward to it. Eli was adapting to being human quite well. He had been mostly human before anyway. He said the hardest adjustment was sleeping. He felt cheated out of hours of the day. Welcome to my world, I told him.

While we were making our way to lunch, Eli held the door open for me, but something in the corner caught my eye. I looked under Eli's arm to see Tate and some girl in the corner. They were making out unabashedly and I felt sorry for him. He apparently was hell bent on drowning his sorrows by using any girl who came his way. You just couldn't help people who didn't want it.

In the cafeteria, Dee searched frantically for someone, and I could guess who. We moseyed into the lunch line when I saw her beeline for the hall. Then her shriek of anger carried to us. It may have been wrong, but there was only one word I could think of for someone like her, who used people and took what she wanted only to find herself on the opposite side.

Karma.

Epilogue

"Clara Hopkins," the announcer called and I made my way across the stage. I smiled at Mrs. Ruth and Pastor as they snapped photos and I held my diploma up.

I did it.

I made my way back down and waited. The Ts would be a while still.

So I thought about where I was going the next day. Eli was taking me somewhere as a surprise, somewhere that required packed bags and a talk with Pastor and Mrs. Ruth about me being gone for a while. They seemed reserved, but understood that this was just the way things were. I was about to be eighteen in a few days and with prom and graduation behind us, we were empty pages waiting to be filled.

"Elijah Thames," the announcer called and I jerked up to watch him. As he came across I knew what this meant to him. He'd never graduated from any school he'd ever been to. He was human now and this diploma meant something.

When all of our friends, Mrs. Ruth and Pastor started to cheer, he jolted in surprise as if he hadn't expected anyone to. I held my diploma under my arm, cupped my mouth and yelled loudly for him. He grinned as he came off stage and pulled me to him. He swung me around gently before putting my feet on the floor again. "Well?" I asked. "How does it feel?"

"It feels like I thought it would." He pressed his lips to my ear. "Like I'm glad that you're finally graduated so I can get you out of this town."

I giggled. Me, too.

"Will you go out with me tonight, love?" he asked as seriousness took over. "I know it's your last night here, and I won't keep you long, but I really wanted to talk to you about something before we left town."

"Yeah, sure."

"Good." He pressed his forehead to mine. "I love you."

"I love you, too."

He nodded behind me. "Pastor."

They hugged me, too, and I told them I was going with Eli for a bit, but would definitely be home soon for some 'family' time before I left.

Family time...

~ ~ ~

Eli and I drove his car down to the quarry. He seemed happy and a little smile sat on his lips the whole drive. When we got out, he grabbed a blanket from the back seat and took me to the dock. After spreading it out, we leaned back on it, but he sat back up and reached into his bag. He tossed me a green apple and bit into his.

"So…" I started and twiddled the apple in my fingers. "Apparently someone made a rather large anonymous donation to the bank to cover the church and the parish's mortgages. Mrs. Ruth was all crying and hallelujahing about it last night. Isn't that the strangest thing?"

"Weird," he muttered and bit into his apple. He grinned in his peripheral as he chewed. He threw the core into the lake, wiping his hands on his jeans. "I've got something for you."

"What's that?"

"This," he whispered and pulled it from his pocket. I knew instantly it was a ring without him having to say it. "I bought it when we got back, but I thought Pastor wouldn't appreciate the gesture just yet."

I laughed breathlessly. "You're right about that."

"But now, I want you to wear it." He took my hand in his. "I want it to be known to everyone that you're mine."

I fingered the string still attached to us. "If they could see this, they'd know."

"But only you and I can see it," he said and held the ring for me to see. It was a beautiful circular setting. Not too big, but not nonexistent either. "You did say yes. May I?"

"You better," I joked and grinned in anticipation. I went to remove my mom's ring, but he stopped me.

"No, don't. Wear them both…until you don't need to keep that promise to your mom anymore."

I stilled. What other guy would ever say something like that? "Thank you," I said and swallowed the tears. "Hopefully, it'll be soon right?"

His smile was all human male and I laughed as he slid the ring on in front of my mom's promise ring and hugged me to him. "Not long. I can't wait for you to be mine in every way…" he said suggestively, but then grinned, "even on paper." I slapped his arm and laughed. "Were you thinking I was talking about another way, CB?"

I giggled. "Oh, so now *I'm* the perv?"

"I guess so."

We laughed and giggled as we lay on the dock. Then he rolled me under him and looked down at me. "There is something I wanted to tell you." He leaned forward, kissing my neck, and then touched his lips to my ear. "I made a little discovery that I wanted to share with you."

"Ok," I whispered cautiously, but then we were on a beach. I sat up, pushing Eli off into the sand. He laughed at my shock. "How did you-"

"It must have stuck. Maybe it was a gift for being such a willing sacrifice?" He smiled. "Who cares? We got to keep your favorite thing about me being a Devourer."

"But what about the rest? What if you can-"

He slipped his hand behind my neck and pulled me to his lips. After some convincing with those lips - and that tongue ring - he pulled back, but not far. "I tested everything. This is the only thing that remains with the bond string. I don't know why, but I don't care." He frowned. "I thought you'd be happy?"

"I am," I said breathlessly, "I'm just shocked. You've done so well at adjusting to being completely human. It just seems almost…foreign for you to have this ability still."

"There's that word again. Foreign," he said playfully with a cocked pierced brow.

I leaned forward and smoothed it with my fingers. "I'm happy." He closed his eyes. "How long have you known?"

"Since this morning. I really wanted to see you and it just sort of popped into my mind. I just came to you for a second, but it was enough." His eyes opened and he looked as if he remembered something. He pulled the collar of my shirt down. "How's this doing?"

"Almost completely gone now."

He moved over and ran his thumb over the brand on my heart. "And this?"

My breath hitched and I squeaked. "Good."

He smiled a genuine smile and cupped my face as he kissed me gently, but long and thorough.

On a beach.

In a reverie.

With my human.

~ ~ ~

We'd driven all day and night to reach this secret destination. He looked sexy and right in his car as we rode with the windows down. His hair moved with the wind and his aviators sat on his face handsomely.

He pulled into a little dirt road. It was wooded and secluded. I looked at him, wondering if he knew just how much of a non-camping girl I was. He smiled in his peripheral as if he could read my thoughts and pulled the car under some trees.

We got out and while Eli made a call, I fiddled anxiously with my beaded bracelet that sat on top of the bond on my wrist. I heard a ringtone somewhere around us and moved to Eli's side. We were in the backwoods of Mississippi for goodness sake. Then someone emerged from the brush. Franz?

"Eli. Clara, welcome."

I looked at Eli in question. He said, "They moved. The rebel camps are always on the move."

"The whole camp is here? Bridgette?" I said hopefully.

He nodded. "I thought you might want to see them again and they definitely wanted to see you. The illustrious girl who tamed a Devourer." He smiled wryly. "I think I'm just a consolation prize."

I felt myself frown. "Why do they care about me though?"

"Because we were in their shoes." He shrugged. "None of them should be friends according to our supernatural world, and they know we understand-Well…understood, I guess. It no longer applies since I'm human now."

"That's where you're wrong," Franz told him. "The new Horde has been assembled and they've already started to look for you again. They know you left Montana, but they didn't know where."

He paled and gripped my fingers tighter. "Why do they care about me now? I'm human?"

"You're the worst kind of abomination, Eli." He looked at me in apology. "You became what they use and despise."

"So we're on the run. Again," Eli said angrily.

"Join us, Eli," Franz said vehemently. "Join us! We could always use a few extra hands in the rebel cause. We'll keep you safe."

"But why would you do that? The Horde is a Devourer problem."

"Well, not only because we have Devourers in our camp, but also because we've been in your shoes. We've all been chased by someone who thought we shouldn't be who or what we are. But together, with all our mixed knowledge and powers and minds, we're stronger than them."

Eli looked at me, but I was already smiling. I nodded to him. This was what we were supposed to do; help others like us, in our situation. Fight for our right to love, live and be happy. I nodded again when he stood still.

"This is where we belong."

"The Horde won't stop," Franz told him. "You know they won't."

"I never meant to start a war with them," Eli said to me. "I just wanted you."

"And you have me." I kissed his chin. "And now we have a big family, too."

He looked at Franz who winked at him and grinned. It was all over Eli's face that I was about to get my way. I held in my smug grin. Franz tipped his head towards the woods and we followed him silently. He took us to a camp. There were people walking around and getting plates made for dinner.

They all stopped when we came up. I felt my blush start as they stared…but then they erupted in applause and cheers. They ran to us and welcomed us. I was hugged by creatures I hadn't even see before and told how happy they were that we were there.

Bridgette pushed her way through the crowd and hugged me like we were sisters. Her Devourer came forward, too. They weren't bonded, just mated, and you could tell that he wasn't as sweet and loving as Eli was with me, but he wasn't a jerk like the rest of the Devourers either.

I watched as the Devourer with Eli kept looking back at Bridgette. It wasn't love, it was more like possession, but it was more than just being a mate, too. Interesting.

Eli talked to him while Bridgette filled me in on everything that had happened in the past few weeks, and even started on some camp gossip.

Wow. I was pretty lucky. I had two families now.

Later that night as we ate bowls of soup around a large fire, I looked forward to what was to come; with the rebel camp, with my parents who were safe in Montana since the Horde knew we left, with Eli…

I gripped his fingers as his hand was already wrapped around mine. He looked at me from speaking to someone and I smiled. He looked serious as he said, "Come with me for a minute." He pulled me up from the bench and took me to a little alcove of trees.

I was confused. "Eli, what-"

His lips stopped everything. He put his hand on my cheek and leaned back just enough for him to murmur against my lips, "I love you, Clara."

Even though he gripped my thigh as he pressed me to the tree, pulling my leg up and kissing my lips with fervor as he groaned, I knew I was safe.

In every way.

~ ~ ~

I didn't think I would be one of those fidgeting girls. It was the thought of being in front of all of those people more than the thought of what I was doing. Mrs. Ruth fussed with my hair and I swatted her hand away gently and smiled at her. "You're more nervous than me. Come on, deep breaths."

She sighed and looked around the corner. "Eli has an…extensive family," she said, trying to sound polite. I held in my giggle, just barely, at knowing exactly what and who was out there.

I was barefoot with a plain white slip dress. Mrs. Ruth's pearl earrings hung from my ears and a bouquet Ariel had made from honeysuckle sat in my fidgeting fingers. I was itching with anticipation to peek around and see Eli. We'd said low-key. The guest were wearing casual. It was outside in the park and it couldn't have been a more beautiful day. I glanced up and looked around me, taking deep breaths.

There was a cloud rabbit above me and it seemed to seam the threads of our fates together even as this day was doing just that. I smiled.

"What?" Mrs. Ruth said and looked up. "Is there a bird's nest? They'll poop on your dress!"

"No," I laughed and gripped her hand. "It's nothing."

Then we heard the music. As if my eyes had been waiting for that one note to sound, they filled with happy tears. This was it. As Patrick's guitar strummed an acoustic version of Red's "You Are Not Alone", and his tenor carried the words through the park, Mrs. Ruth wound her arm through mine and we turned the stone wall corner. The rebel camp was there, every single one of them. The church congregation was there, too.

It had been a short engagement. Two weeks after graduation, we could wait no longer and caved. We spilled our plans to Pastor and Mrs. Ruth, who both seemed not-so-surprised by the news. They arranged a very low-key and simple wedding, which was what I wanted more than anything, and four weeks later there we were. All of our family was there, no bridesmaids to fuss with, no grooms to buy tuxes for, no seating charts, no caviar or photographers or coordinators. Just us and our family as they watched us say that we would love each other forever, however long that may be.

I had been worried about the Horde since we learned that they reformed. I wanted to do the Justice of the Peace thing, but Franz was having none of that. He insisted on a wedding where my family could come and that with the whole rebel camp there, there was no way the Horde would make a move. Eli had taken the opportunity to remove all of his funds from the banks as well. He had it stashed in all sorts of places with all sorts of people, but at least it was available to us, and the rebels, and wasn't traceable.

Franz smiled and winked at me as I passed him. Bridgette grinned and wiggled her fingers at me. Ariel bounced on her toes in excitement. I could wait no longer and lifted my gaze to Eli.

His mouth was slightly open as he watched me come towards him. He was wearing khakis and a white button up...along with Enoch. I gasped as I saw him and looked at Eli questionably. He shrugged and smiled. I swung my gaze back to Enoch. He rolled his eyes and huffed in that way that was becoming so familiar. I smiled at him. He would never be like Eli, and probably would never even like me, but he was trying. For his brother. What more could I ask of him?

We arrived and Mrs. Ruth gave me over to Eli's awaiting hand. Pastor was watching me and twisting his lips, trying to hold back tears. I looked away so I wouldn't burst myself. But then I looked at Eli and it seriously didn't help. He tucked my hair behind my ear and smiled that smile. The smile that had me hooked from the moment he walked into my town.

"Ready, Mrs. Thames?" he said happily, his grin infectious and breathtaking.

"Oh, yes," I breathed and laughed a little when he wiped a tear from my cheek with his thumb. "Very much ready."

Within minutes Eli was mine.

He was what my mom would have wanted me to find. He was a creature put on earth to manipulate and hurt, and instead had taught me to really love and feel again. Though I had bound us physically with the string, he had reached into my soul and bound us together long before that.

Eli was the love of my one lifetime and I was now the love of his. The future was uncertain and shaky and foggy, and filled with love that I couldn't wait to explore.

And we were just getting started.

The Very End

For Clara and Eli

Look for Enoch's book, Altered, that continues the story of the Horde and the rebels in 2013

Oh, the thank yous could go on for miles. First off, thank you to my God and my family. To the readers who have picked up this book and my others as well, you are the reason I do this. It's been SO much fun getting to know all different kinds of people from all over the world who have read something of mine. It's humbling in every sense of the word and I thank you for allowing me to be a little piece of your world. You guys are the best and I love to hear from you! You rock!

Shelly's other series that are available

The Significance Series

The Collide Series

The Stealing Grace Series

Smash Into You

Be sure to find and follow Shelly on these avenues for updates and information regarding upcoming books and sneak peeks.

www.facebook.com/shellycranefanpage
www.twitter.com/authshellycrane
www.shellycrane.blogspot.com

Playlist

Paradise : Coldplay
Philadelphia : Parachute
Sweet Resistance : Civil Twilight
Hostage : Jack's Mannequin
Absolutely Still : Better Than Ezra
Run For Your Life : The Fray
Green Eyes : Coldplay
Truth : Jason Reeves
My Stupid Mouth : John Mayer
I Can Barely Say : The Fray
Everything :Tyler Ward
Homesick : Sleeping At Last
Ghost In Love : Mikey Wax
Fidelity :Regina Spektor
Restless Dream : Jack's Mannequin
Coming Up Strong : Karmin
You Are Not Alone : Red

Made in the USA
Lexington, KY
17 July 2014